Praise for *Goodnight, Nobody:*

"Knight's characters remain touchingly human, thanks to his subtle, if sardonic, sense of humor and his essential authorial decency."
—Amanda Heller, *The Boston Globe*

"Knight's talent is in the details, all the wonderful little moments he hands us along the way. . . . [Each] of Knight's best stories . . . makes you want to retell it to someone, the way you'd describe the plot of a good novel to a friend."
—Anne Stephenson, *USA Today*

"A great collection—Knight is a savvy writer who is serious even as he entertains. . . . The humor that winds its way through this collection is droll, understated and enticing, a welcome mat for people who usually prefer novels to stories."
—*The Arizona Republic*

"From the first pages . . . it's clear that Michael Knight is simply a great writer. Tremendous."   —*Kirkus Reviews* (starred review)

"Michael Knight is more than a master of the short story. He knows the true pace of life and does not cheat it, all the while offering whopping entertainment."   —Barry Hannah

"[Knight is] skilled at observing what makes people tick and what makes them trip, and [presents] singular dispatches from life's odd corners, polishing simple words until they shine like plain stones run through a rock tumbler."
—Kevin Allman, *The Washington Post Book World*

"Funny and poignant . . . 'Birdland' is in itself worth the price of the book." —Barbara Quick, *San Francisco Chronicle*

"Every story in *Goodnight, Nobody* is perfect. Michael Knight is a talented enough writer to tell any kind of tale he wants, but he's at his best when he's exploring this question: What happens to good men when they have lost just enough of their dignity, love and hope to take some wild gamble to retrieve all three at once?" —Elizabeth Gilbert

"A must read. . . . The stories of *Goodnight, Nobody* move with such fluidity, such effortless pace, that this brilliant new collection should be read twice: once for the sheer pleasure of it, and once more to soak up the careful artistry of Michael Knight's prose." —*The Virginia Quarterly Review*

"As each tale unfolds we meet people who are exceptional because they are willing to take chances: on love, for family, for a better life. . . . Knight makes the most of characters with little or nothing going for them. His characters discover their mettle in everyday struggles." —Ginny Merdes, *The Seattle Times*

"Skillful . . . The first thing one notices is the intelligence and beauty of Knight's sentences . . . how textured Knight's writing is. . . . [He] uses humor to free the reader from any forced sympathizing, and instead of watering down a story's impact, humor becomes a kind of enabling restraint. . . . There is much to admire here." —Tommy Hays, *The Atlanta Journal-Constitution*

"Powerful . . . The words fall on the page like whispers and the tone is subdued. . . . Knight's stories are nights by the hearth with a blanket thrown over and scratchy jazz records playing on the turntable nearby."   —Jonathan Shipley, Bookreporter.com

"[Knight's] stories strike a rich balance between anxiety and humor, often obscuring an impending crisis behind its outlandish peculiarities. . . . The plainspoken precision of Knight's best writing suits the colloquial mannerisms of his characters. . . . Knight [has a] talent for shining a sympathetic light on the compromises and failures of the people who inhabit his stories."
                                              —Mark Sorkin, *Rain Taxi*

"[Knight] is an up-and-coming, first-rate short-story writer in the Southern tradition. . . . *Goodnight, Nobody* is sure to captivate all who like well-written fiction."
                                        —Gilbert M. Singer, *Tampa Tribune*

Goodnight, Nobody

Michael Knight

Goodnight, Nobody

Grove Press
New York

The stories in this collection have appeared in the following publications, sometimes in slightly different forms: "Birdland" in *The New Yorker* and *New Stories from the South: The Year's Best, 1999* (Algonquin); "Feeling Lucky" in *Virginia Quarterly Review,* and in *Stories from the South: The Year's Best, 2004;* "Killing Stonewall Jackson" in *Story* and *Stories from the Blue Moon Cafe* (McAdam/Cage); "The End of Everything" in *GQ;* "The Mesmerist" in *Esquire;* "Keeper of Secrets, Teller of Lies" in *Virginia Quarterly Review;* "Ellen's Book" in *Five Points* and *New Stories from the South: The Year's Best, 2003.*

Published simultaneously in Canada
Printed in the United States of America

FIRST GROVE PRESS EDITION

Library of Congress Cataloging-in-Publication Data
Knight, Michael, 1969–
    Goodnight, nobody / by Michael Knight.
        p. cm.
    Contents: Birdland — Feeling lucky — Killing Stonewall Jackson — The end of everything — The mesmerist — Keeper of secrets, teller of lies — Mitchell's girls — Ellen's book — Blackout.
    ISBN 0-8021-4055-6 (pbk.)
    1. Southern States–Social life and customs–Fiction.   I. Title.
PS3561.N486 G66 2002
813'.54—dc21   2002027944

Grove Press
841 Broadway
New York, NY 10003

04 05 06 07 08   10 9 8 7 6 5 4 3 2 1

For Mary

Contents

Birdland

Between the months of April and September, Pawtucket, Rhode Island, is inhabited by several generations of African parrots. A millionaire and philanthropist named Archibald brought a dozen or so over from Kenya around the turn of the century and kept them in an aviary built against the side of his house. A few days before his death, in a moment more notable for generosity than good sense, he swung open the cage and released the birds into a wide summer sky. According to eyewitness reports, the parrots made a dazed circle beneath the clouds, surprised by their sudden freedom, and, not immediately seeing anything more to their liking, lighted amid the branches of an apple orchard on the back acreage of Archibald's property. There, as is the habit of nature, they flourished and have continued to thrive for more than ninety years. But in September, when winter creeps in from the ocean and cold air kindles hazy instincts, the parrots flee south for warmer climes and settle here, in Elbow, Alabama, along a slow bend in the Black Warrior River, where perhaps they are reminded of waters, slower still, in an almost forgotten continent across the sea.

I know all this because The Blond told me it was true. The Blond has platinum hair and round hips and a pair of ornithology degrees from a university up in New Hampshire. She has a given name as well—Ludmilla Haggarsdottir—but no one in town is comfortable with its proper pronunciation. The Blond came to Elbow a year past, researching a book about Archibald's parrots, and was knocked senseless by the late August heat. Even after the weight had gone out of summer and the parrots had arrived and football was upon us, she staggered around in a safari hat and sunglasses, drunk with the fading season, scribbling notes on the progress of the birds. She took pictures and sat sweating in the live-oak shade. They don't have this sort of heat in New Hampshire—bone-warming, inertial heat, humidity thick enough to slow your blood. She rented a room in my house, the only room for rent in town. At night, we would sit on the back porch, fireflies blundering against the screen, and make love on my grandmother's old daybed. "Tell me a story, Raymond," The Blond would say. "Tell me something I've never heard before." The Blond is not the only one with a college education. "This," I said, throwing her leg over my shoulder, "is how Hector showed his love to Andromache the night before Achilles killed him dead."

The only TV for thirty miles sits on the counter at Dillard's Country Store. Dillard has a gas pump out front and all the essentials inside, white bread and yellow mustard and cold beer. Dillard himself brews hard cider and doubles as mayor of Elbow. He is eighty-one years old and has been unanimously elected to eleven consecutive terms. On fall Saturdays, all of Elbow gathers in his store to watch the Alabama team take the field, me and The Blond and the mayor and Mae and Wilson Camp, who have a soybean farm north of town. Lookout Mountain Coley is the nearest thing we have to a local celebrity. These days, he stocks shelves in the grocery and mans the counter when the mayor is in the head, but thirty-five years ago, he was only the second black man to play football for the great Bear Bryant and once returned a punt ninety-nine yards for a touchdown against Tennessee. The Crimson Tide is not what it used to be, however, and we all curse God for commandeering our better days. Leonard and Chevy Foote, identical twins, have the foulest mouths in Elbow, their dialogue on game day nothing more than a long string of invective against blind referees and unfair recruiting practices and dumbass coaches who aren't fit to wipe Bear Bryant's behind. The parrots perch in pecan trees beyond the open windows and listen to us rant. At night, with the river curving slow and silent, they mimic us in the dark. "Catch the ball," they caw in Mayor Dillard's desperate falsetto, "Catch the ball, you stupid nigger." Mayor Dillard is an unrepentant racist and I often wonder what the citizens of Pawtucket, Rhode Island, must think when the birds leave us in the spring.

The Blond is still working on her book. She follows the birds from tree to tree, keeping an eye on reproductive habits and the condition of winter plumage. Parrot, she tells me, is really just a catch-all name for several types of birds, such as the macaw, the cockatoo, the lory, and the budgerigar. Common to all genera, including our African grays, are a hooked bill, a prehensile tongue, and yoke-toed claws. The African parrot can live up to eighty years, she says, and often mates for life, though our local birds have apparently adopted a more swinging sexual culture due to an instinctive understanding of the rigors of perpetuation in a nonindigenous environment. Her book will be about the insistence of nature. It will be about surviving against the odds. One day, says The Blond, she will return to Pawtucket, as she had originally planned, and resume her studies there. She mentions this when she is angry with me for one reason or another and leads me to her room, where her suitcase still sits packed atop my grandmother's antique bureau. And the thought of her leaving does frighten me to good behavior. I can hardly remember what my life was like without her here, though I managed fine a long time before she arrived. Seven months ago, when March finally brought her to her senses and the birds began to filter north, The Blond and I were already too tangled up for her to leave.

My grandmother left me this house upon her death. It isn't a big house, just a one-story frame number with a sleeping porch and a converted attic, which is I where I make my bed, but it sits high on red clay bluffs and when November rain has stripped leaves from the trees, you can see all the way to the Black Warrior. Here, the river bends like a folded arm, which is how our town came to have its name. In the fall, while we sit mesmerized and enraged by the failings of our team, the dark water litters Dillard Point with driftwood and detritus, baby carriages and coat hangers, kites, and high-heeled shoes. When the game has ended and I need an hour to collect myself, I wander Mayor Dillard's land, collecting branches that I carve into parrot figurines and sell from a shelf in the window of his store. We have bird-watchers by the busload in season and, outside of the twenty dollars a month I charge The Blond for room and board, these whittlings account for my income. But I don't need much in the way of money anymore. Years ago, my family owned a lumber mill and a loading dock by the river so the company could ship wood to Mobile. My great-grandfather torched the mill in 1939 for insurance and gradually, a few at a time, people drifted downstream for work until there was almost no one left. The Blond wonders why we still bother with elections since there are fewer than a dozen voters and Dillard always wins. I tell her we believe in democracy in Alabama. I tell her we have faith in the American way.

Neither does The Blond understand our commitment to college football. Ever the scientist, she has theorized that a winning team gives us a reason to take pride in being from Alabama and with our long history of bigotry and oppression and our more recent dismal record in public education and environmental conservation, such reasons, according to The Blond, are few and far between. I don't know whether or not she is correct, but I suspect that she is beginning to recognize the appeal of the Crimson Tide. Just last week, as we watched Alabama in a death struggle with the Florida Gators, our halfback fumbled and she jerked out of her chair, her fists closed tight, her breasts bouncing excitedly. She had to clench her jaw to keep from calling out. Her face was glazed with sweat, the fine hairs on her upper lip visible in the dusty light. The sight of her like that, all balled-up enthusiasm, her shirt knotted beneath her ribs, sweat pooling in the folds of her belly, moved me to dizziness. I held her hand and led her out onto the porch. Dillard's store is situated at a junction of rural highways and we watched a tour bus rumble past, eager old women hanging from the windows with binoculars at their eyes. The pecan trees were dotted with parrots, blurs of brighter red and smears of gray in among the leaves. "Catch the ball," one called out and another answered, "Stick him like a man, you fat country bastard." She sat on the plank steps and I knelt at her bare feet. "Will you marry me?" I said. "You are a prize greater than Helen of Troy." She looked at me sadly for a minute, her hand going clammy in mine. The game was back on inside, an announcer's voice floating through the open door. After a while she said, "I can't live here the rest of my life." She stood and went back inside to watch the rest of the game, which we lost on a last-second Hail Mary pass that broke all our hearts at once.

The Blond won't sleep a whole night with me. She slips up the drop ladder to my attic and we wind together in the dark, her body pale above me, moonlight catching in her movie star hair. When she is finished, she smokes cigarettes at the gable window and I tell her stories about the Trojan War. I explain how the Greeks almost lost everything when Achilles and Agamemnon argued over a woman. I tell her that male pride is a volatile energy, some feathers better left unruffled, but she only likes the stories for background noise. She is more interested in the parrots, a few of whom have taken up roost in an oak tree beside my house. If there is a full moon, the birds are awake for hours, calling, "Who are you?" back and forth in the luminous night; "Why are you in my house?" According to The Blond, old Archibald was deep in Alzheimer's by the time of his death and was unable even to recognize his own children when they visited. She goes dreamy-eyed imagining the parrots passing these words from generation to generation. Before she returns to her bed, she wonders aloud why it is that the birds learned such existential phrases in Rhode Island and such ugly, bitter words down here.

Sometimes, Lookout Mountain Coley gets fed up with Mayor Dillard shouting "nigger" at the TV screen. Having played for Alabama in the halcyon sixties, Lookout knows what football means to people around here and he restrains himself admirably. But when they were younger men and Mayor Dillard crossed whatever invisible boundary exists between them, Lookout would circle his fists in the old style and challenge him to a fight. They'd roll around in the dirt parking lot a while, sweat running muddy on their skin. Nowadays, he presses his lips together and his face goes blank and hard like he is turning himself to stone. He walks outside without a word, watches the birds across the highway. He wolf-whistles, the way the parrots are supposed to, and speaks to them in ordinary phrases. "Pretty bird, pretty bird. How about a little song?" After a few minutes, Mayor Dillard shakes his head and joins Lookout beside the road, 142 years of life between them. We focus our attention on the game so they can have some time alone to sort things out. No one knows for sure what goes on between them out there, but they return patting each other on the back, making promises that neither of them will keep. Mayor Dillard offers a public apology each time, says he hopes the people of Elbow won't hold this incident against him come election. He buys a round of bottled beers and Lookout accepts the apology with grace, waving his beer at the TV so we'll quit looking at him and keep our minds on simpler things.

Her first season in town, The Blond was appalled by these displays. She is descended from liberal-minded Icelandic stock, and she couldn't understand why Lookout or any of us would allow

Mayor Dillard to go on the way he does. She sprang to her feet and clicked off the television and delivered an angry lecture welcoming us to the "twentieth-fucking-century." Her fury was gorgeous, her face red, her thighs quivering righteously beneath her hiking shorts. She tried to convince Lookout to report Mayor Dillard to the NAACP and, short of that, to run for mayor himself, arguing that because he was a minor sports celebrity he might have the clout to unseat an incumbent. But Lookout told her he wasn't interested. He shook his head gravely and said, "Uneasy is the head that wears the ground, miss." Though I know she would be loath to admit it, the words don't offend her so much anymore. You can get used to anything, given time. Some nights, however, when she is moving violently over me, she grits her teeth and says, "Who's the nigger, Raymond? Who's the nigger now?" I understand that her indignation is not aimed directly at me, but that doesn't make those nights any easier. I twist myself sleeplessly in the sheets when she is gone.

Raymond was my father's name. I am the only child of a land surveyor. My mother died giving birth and my dad wandered farther and farther afield looking for work until, finally, he never returned. I was thirteen when he disappeared, left here with my grandmother and the house. She paid for my education with nickels and dimes, millions of them, hidden in Mason jars beneath her bed because hers were old notions and she trusted neither banks nor the long-term value of paper money. "That's ancient history," she said, when I told her what I was studying. "You ought to be thinking about the future." She loved this town and hoped that I would bring my learning home and give something back. She made me promise before she died. But all I have given unto Elbow is driftwood parrots and The Blond. Everyone knows she lingers here because of me and no one is quite sure how they feel about that.

A few days ago, she found a parrot nest in Wilson Camp's defunct grain silo and spent a whole day sitting against the wall, watching the mother feed her babies regurgitated pecans. I panicked when I returned from wandering Dillard Point and found an empty house, waited on the porch and watched the road for cars but she never showed. I don't have a phone so I drove from house to house, stopped by to see Lookout, swung past the Footes' mobile home, whipped the town into a posse. I prowled country lanes until I saw her Jeep parked beside the Camps' most distant field. When I didn't spot her right away, I suspected the worst. This deserted road and vacant field are like horror movie sets, the silo rising from the ground like a wizard's tower. I called her name but only the parrots answered back. "Who are you?" Their voices were flat and distant. "Catch the ball." Then, faintly, I heard her voice, a stage whisper coming from the silo and when I crawled in beside her, she shined a flashlight on the nest and I could see the baby birds, their feathers still slick and insufficient, heads wobbly on their necks. The Blond threw her arms around me and wept and pressed her lips against my collarbone.

Mayor Dillard has a deal with his counterpart in Pawtucket, Rhode Island. On one Saturday in the fall and one in spring the towns combine in celebrating Parrot Days. In October, the mayor of Pawtucket flies south on his constituents' tab. He stands outside the store where Lookout has rigged a hand-painted banner, delivers a short speech, and has his picture snapped for the record, his limousine idling beside the grandstand. Then he continues on to New Orleans, where he spends a few days whoring and playing at being a bigwig. Dillard takes a similar trip in May, which we do not begrudge him, and winds up in Atlantic City; once, Lookout had to drive up there to bail him out of jail. Our octogenarian mayor, it seems, was chasing showgirls down a hotel hallway wearing only an Indian headdress and screeching "Polly want a cracker" at the top of his lungs. Such, I suppose, are the prerogatives of power.

Mayor Dillard always arranges it so that Parrot Days fall during an off week for the Crimson Tide. This year, we gather in the parking lot and offer gifts to the Pawtucket delegation, my figurines and jugs of hard cider and a red plastic hat shaped like an elephant head, and listen to the visiting mayor give his speech. The parrots jeer him from the trees. "Run, darkie, run," they call and he pretends not to notice. The Blond is disappointed with the day. She wanted more from these proceedings, wanted something meaningful and real, but most of us are grateful for a break from football this year. Six games into the season and already we've lost four. Another stinker and Bama is out of contention for a bowl. We'd settle for anything at this point: Taco Bell Aloha, Sun America Copper, even the Poulan Weed Eater over in Louisiana.

Elbow, Alabama, is easy enough to find. Take Highway 14 north from Sherwood until you come to Easy Money Road. Bear east and keep driving until you're sure you've gone too far. Past a red barn with the words "His desire shall be satisfied upon the hills of Gilead" painted on the planks in gold letters, past a field where no crops will grow, past a cypress split by lightning and full of vivid, loquacious birds. This is modest country and nature has had her steady way for years. My house is just a little farther, over a hill, left on the gravel drive. Someone filched the mailbox years ago, but the post is still standing, headless and crooked. All our mail is addressed to Dillard's Country Store. In the evenings, when the sun dangles like molten glass over the river, we ride into town and Mayor Dillard presents us with news from the world. Once a month, the Footes hang their heads and grit their teeth, a stew of shame and desire running in their veins because their subscription to *Titty* has arrived. The Camps get postcards now and then from Wilson's brother, Max, and his other brother, Andre, whose marriage broke up years ago. Lookout gets religious pamphlets and sports recruiting news, but letters never come for me. I no longer have connections beyond the boundaries of our town. The Blond dawdles nearby when Mayor Dillard passes out the mail, her hair sweat-damp against her neck. She cracks her knuckles and goes for nonchalance. She has, it seems, applied for a government grant. She wrote the proposal without telling me and will head north in spring if her funding comes through on time. We are sitting at a picnic table behind my house eating PB&J when she announces her intentions. I force down a mouthful, ask her to marry me a second time but her answer is the same. She covers my hand with hers, looks an apology across the table. The Blond holds all of history against me. When it is clear that I have nothing else to say, she stands and walks around the front of the house. I find her staring up into the trees at a pair of fornicating parrots. "Don't mistake this for love," she tells the birds. "Don't be talked into something you'll regret." She watches unblinking, her arms crossed at her chest, her vigorous legs shoulder-width apart. I ask her why she stayed last spring, why she didn't follow the parrots when they left Elbow for the season. She tells me she was broke, that's all. She would have vanished if she'd had the cash. I remind her that she paid her rent, that she was never short of cigarettes and oils for her hair. "Shut up," says The Blond. "I know what you want to hear."

When I was fourteen, Hurricane Frederick whipped in from the Gulf of Mexico, spinning tornadoes upriver as far as Elbow. Dillard's store was pancaked and a sixty-foot pine fell across the roof of my grandmother's house. My father had been gone almost a year and we huddled in the pantry, the old woman and I, and listened to the wind moving room to room like a search party. The next day, she sent me to town on foot to borrow supplies and see if everyone was all right. Telephone poles were stacked along the road like pickup sticks. But the most terrifying thing of all was the quiet. The parrots were gone, the trees without pigment and voice. We thought they had all been killed and, to this day, no one is certain where they spent the winter, though The Blond has unearthed testimony for her book regarding strange birds sighted in the panhandle of Florida during the last months of 1979. We rebuilt the grocery and my grandmother turned her roof repairs into a party, serving up cheese and crackers and a few bottles of champagne she'd saved from her wedding. Despite our efforts at good cheer and exempting New Year's Day when Bear Bryant licked Joe Paterno in the Sugar Bowl, a pall hung over town until Lookout spotted the birds coming back, dozens of them coloring the sky like a ticker tape parade.

Our river is named for the Indian chief Tuscaloosa, which means Black Warrior in Choctaw, and when I was a boy you could find arrowheads and chips of pottery buried in the banks. Now, as I make my way along the shore, the river offers up Goodyear radials and headless Barbie dolls. Parrots dance from branch to branch above me. I remember Calypso casting a spell to keep Odysseus on her island and I want to teach the birds a phrase so full of magic The Blond will never leave. At night, she types her notes and files them away on the chance the government will respond to her request. It's warm enough still, even in October, that we leave the windows open, air grazing her skin and carrying her scent to my chair in the next room. I whittle and listen to sports radio and wish I had a phone so I could call all the broadcasters in New Jersey who have forgotten how great we used to be, how we won a dozen National Championships, how Alabama lost only six games in the first ten years of my life. To listen to them talk, you'd think they never heard Bear Bryant was on a stamp. I pace the floor when I get agitated and shuffle wood shavings with my feet. I talk back to my grandmother's Motorola portable. When I make the fierce turn toward my chair, I see The Blond standing in the doorway, her hands on the frame above her. She smiles and shakes her head. "You people," she says. "When are you gonna put all that Bear Bryant stuff behind you? That's all dead and gone." I cross myself Catholic-style and look at her a long moment, my heart tiny in my chest. She is wearing a man's sleeveless undershirt and boxer shorts, her hair pinned behind her head with a pencil. I would forgive her almost any sacrilege for the length of her neck or the way she rests one foot on top of the other and curls her painted toes. "I thought you liked football," I say. She crosses the room and puts her hands on my cheeks, kisses the spot between my eyebrows.

I want to tell her that the past is not only for forgetting. There are some things, good and bad, that you shouldn't leave behind. According to the record books, Bear Bryant didn't sign a black player until 1970 because the state of Alabama was not ready for gridiron integration. A decade earlier, however, he recruited a group of Negro running backs who were light-skinned enough to pass for white. They hid their Afros beneath helmets and bunked in a special dorm miles away from campus. They were listed in the program under names Bear himself selected. Lookout Coley's playing name was Patrick O'Reilly.

Every now and then, Mayor Dillard will set his ancient reel-to-reel on a card table and show black-and-white movies of Lookout's punt return against the rear wall of his store. He ordered the game from a sports memorabilia company and we sit in the grass after dark, watch the image break around chips in the paint, press beer bottles against our necks to ward away the heat. There is Lookout, sleek and muscled and young, ball dropping into his arms, shifting his hips side to side, giving a Tennessee defender a stiff-arm to take your breath away. The image flickers as he shakes and shimmies toward the sideline, then he breaks upfield, his back arched with speed, the rest of the world falling away behind him. The movie is without sound and Mayor Dillard rewinds the touchdown over and over, Lookout, streaking backward in front of the Alabama bench past his exultant teammates and granite-faced Bear Bryant, then forward again toward the endzone, all swift and silent grace. None of us has ever done anything so wonderful in all our lives. Chevy Foote whispers like he has witnessed a cosmic event. "Old number 41, man, you sure could fly." Crickets murmur in the underbrush. Lookout weeps quietly and Mayor Dillard throws an arm over his shoulder while the film clicks softly and plays itself out against the backdrop night.

I ask The Blond why the parrots keep returning to Elbow and she says it's instinct, plain and simple. We are sitting on the riverbank with our feet in the water. The Blond slips into her academic's voice as she tells me that because the birds are native to equatorial Africa, because their food supply of seeds, nuts, and fruit dries up in the Rhode Island cold, they are obliged to embark on a southerly migration in order to survive. "It's a miracle *Psittacus eritacus* endures in this country at all," she says and lies back on the ground, crossing her hands behind her neck. There is a parrot perched on a cypress branch across the river watching us with the side of his head. I find a stone on the bank and skip it across the water in his direction and he screeches and flutters his wings at me. "Run, darkie, run," it says. "Why are you in my house?" The Blond squenches her lips disapprovingly and closes her eyes and I run a fingertip along her hairline until the furrows in her brow go smooth. "But why here?" I say. "They could live anywhere in the world." The Blond lifts herself up on her forearm, her hair falling over her eyes, and opens her mouth to speak before she realizes that, for once, she doesn't have an answer to my question.

In the second quarter of the Ole Miss game, a freshman quarterback named Algernon Marquez comes off the bench for Alabama

and throws a pair of touchdowns before the half. For nine minutes, as our team works to tie the score, we are beside ourselves,
leaping about Dillard's Country Store, pitching our bodies into
each other's arms, but at the break, we fall silent, fearing a jinx,
and cross our fingers and apologize to God for all the nasty things
we have said about him in the recent past. Even The Blond wants
to bear the suspense in quiet. She carries her cigarettes outside
and sits smoking in her Jeep. I stand behind my parrot sculptures,
watch her through the window, as she eyes real birds across the road
and pretends she is above all this. But I know otherwise. The Black
Warrior winds forty miles down from Tuscaloosa and The Blond
is hearing faint cheers on the watery wind. The second half, God
bless, belongs to Alabama. Our defense is inspired, our offense
fleet and strong. Algernon Marquez isn't Joe Namath, but he is
more a dream than we could have hoped, "a no-name wonder
from Letohatchee," says the announcer, "whose only goal in life
was to play for the Crimson Tide." I wonder how it would feel to
have achieved all your aspirations by your eighteenth year. A bus
full of Delaware parrot lovers rolls up while the score is 35–17
and Mayor Dillard gives them whatever they want for free.

   That night, I tell The Blond Andromache's story—how,
after Hector's death, she was made a slave to Pyrrhus, the son of
Achilles, but grew to love him a little over time. "She was happy
in his house even though she never guessed it could be true," I
say, sitting on the bed with my back propped up. The Blond is
naked, still flushed from our coupling. "I'm pregnant," she says.
"I can feel it in my bones." She traces concentric circles on her
stomach with a finger, the parrots frantic beyond the windows.
The Blond bolts upright and looks at me, like she wants to see
something behind my eyes. I'm just about to haul her into my
arms and waltz her joyously around the room, when she slaps my
face, leaving an echo in my head. I watch, too stunned to stop
her, while she jumps up and down on the wood floor, landing
hard and flat-footed each time, shaking window panes, sending

ripples along the backs of her legs. She is crying and pounding her knees, and I wrap my arms around her and pin her down. "This is not my baby," she says. "This is not my life," and she keeps shouting until her voice is gone and she has cried herself to sleep beneath me.

There are ghosts in Elbow. Little Hound, one of Chief Tuscaloosa's lieutenants, was betrayed on the banks of our river by Hernando de Soto and his men, shot in the belly, according to legend, then flayed while he was still alive as an example to the Choctaw people. On cold nights, when football season has come and gone, you can hear him chanting a curse against white men in the dark. That old broken-down house on Route 16, the one with the stove-in porch and kudzu creeping up the walls, Gantry Pound murdered his wife and three daughters there because he believed that women were vile creatures and he couldn't bear the smell of their menstruation. According to Wilson and Mae Camp, who live in the next house down the road, an ebullient sorority of phantoms roams the halls at midnight, glad to have the place finally to themselves. Even my house has a ghost. My grandmother swore that she would never leave and sometimes, when I am hovering on the brink of sleep, I see her watching over me, calling me by my father's name, though I am never sure if I am dreaming.

The day after The Blond declared herself with child, just before I open my eyes, I hear a voice, faint as electricity, but the room is empty. Morning finds me alone, still sleeping on the floor. I check the house to be sure, but The Blond is nowhere to be found. Her suitcase is gone from the bureau, her hair care products vanished from the shelf beside the bathroom sink. I sit drinking coffee on the sleeping porch while the parrots call around me. "Who are you? Why are you in my house?" It is not quite new day yet and I watch the world come to life, winter buds opening in the light, the river far below hauling water toward the sea. I tell myself that I will give up hope at lunch. And, though I hold off eating until two o'clock, I keep my promise and carry a melancholy peanut butter sandwich out into the yard. The grass is cool on the bottoms of my feet. I wonder about The Blond, see her streaming down the highway in her Jeep, sunglasses on her head to keep the hair out of her eyes, wonder if she will put an end to our baby in a sterile clinic or if she only wants to get some distance between history and the child. I want to tell her that even bland Ohio is haunted by its crimes. I want to tell her, while the air is full of birds and the shadow of my house still lingers on the yard, that she is exactly what I need. Behind me, as if on cue, The Blond says, "I drove all night, but I didn't know where else to go." I turn to face her, blood jumping in my veins. There are tired blue crescents under her eyes and her hair is knotted from the wind. She smiles and smooths the front of her shorts. I am so grateful I do not have the strength to speak. "I took a pee test in Gadsden," she says. "It's official." The Blond walks over, grabs my wrist, and guides my sandwich to her lips.

Election day is nearing again, November 17. Though he will, as usual, run unopposed, Mayor Dillard is superstitious about complacency. He pays Lookout overtime to haul campaign buttons out of the storage shed behind his store and stake *Dillard Does It Better* signs along the road. He visits each of his constituents in person, bribes us with hard cider and the promise of a brighter future here in Elbow. Bird-watching is up, crime down, he tells us at his fried chicken fund-raiser, and each will continue in the appropriate direction if he is reelected. Things are looking brighter for the Alabama team as well. We've won two games in a row and all the Yankee radio personalities are beginning to see the light. They say our team has an outside shot at the Peach Bowl over in Georgia, where we will likely face Virginia's Cavaliers. But we do not speak a word of this in town. We hold our breath and say our prayers because hated Auburn is still looming in the distance and one false step could bring all this new hope down around us like a house of cards. At night, The Blond and I drink nonalcoholic beverages beneath the Milky Way. We have reached an acceptable compromise: spring in Rhode Island, fall back here, until she is finished with her study, but she will give birth in Alabama. Elbow will have a new voter in eighteen years and The Blond has convinced Lookout to contend for mayor himself one day. He will not run against his friend, he says. Too much has passed between them. But it won't be long before Mayor Dillard gives in to time, and Lookout Mountain Coley can sweep injustice from our town like an Old West sheriff. My life purls drowsily out behind me like water. Parrots preen invisibly in the dark. I shuttle inside for more ice and listen to The Blond spin stories about our unborn child. Her daughter, she says, will discover a lost tribe of parrots in the wilds of Borneo and invent a vaccine for broken hearts. She will write a novel so fine no other books need writing anymore, and she will marry, if she chooses, an imperfect man and make him good inside. And maybe, if the stars are all in line, our daughter will grow up to be the hardest-hitting free safety who ever lived.

Feeling Lucky

Midnight, and Bruce Little was hunched against a pay phone under the awning of the Saint John Divine Hotel, shivering with cold and dialing collect to Mississippi. He called twice. No answer either time. This was February. This was Richmond. His daughter, Jane, was in the room asleep. His ex-wife, Barbara, was in Teaneck, New Jersey, with her new husband, worrying, he supposed, about Jane and hoping for good news from the police. He'd put eleven hours of road between them. Before that, he'd waited behind the hedge until Jane came out to build a snowman, then plucked her over the back fence when Barbara went inside to use the can. Now, he was impatient with fatigue. He counted the money in his wallet—nine one-dollar bills. He forced himself to smoke a cigarette to the filter before he dialed again. The operator cut in when the answering machine picked up.

The Saint John Divine was four stories, brownstone, maybe three dozen rooms. In another life, it had probably been a decent place, with a bellman in livery and an elevator boy, but now the old Otis was shot and the only other guests Bruce had seen were a pair of tipsy fags sneaking a white cat into their room. Bruce had a soft spot for places like this—local, half-dead, unashamed. He'd spent his share of nights in hotels since his divorce. This one, he'd found by accident. He was low on gas and he left the interstate at random, got snagged in a web of one-way streets. He had wanted to cover more ground, but Jane was fading fast and there was the hotel. Across the street was a church with the same name. He would ask directions back to the interstate in the morning. First, he needed Melinda to answer the phone. Melinda could wire him a little money. Nine dollars wouldn't get him home.

Bruce glared at the phone for a moment, like it was part of a conspiracy to prevent him from completing his call, then headed for the desk to make change. The night manager was perched on a stool behind the counter, watching a TV mounted eight feet above the floor. She was an older woman, maybe seventy, he thought, dyed black hair in a bouffant cloud around her head. A metal screen separated her station from the lobby proper—matching chair and loveseat, both done in plastic, and a coffee table littered with movie magazines. Bruce fingered three singles from his wallet, passed them through the screen. The night manager cashed them in, but didn't hand his quarters over right away.

"Is there something wrong with the phone in your room?" she said.

"Not that I'm aware of," Bruce said.

"If there's something wrong, you should let me know," she said.

"There's nothing wrong," he said.

"Because," she said, "how'm I gonna fix it if I don't know it's broke?"

"It's not broken," he said. "It's just my little girl isn't feeling very well. I didn't want to wake her up." This was true. Jane had started wilting halfway across Pennsylvania. By the time they hit Virginia, she was drifting in and out of sleep, her head wobbling on her neck, stirring just long enough to complain about how she felt—her stomach hurt, it was too cold in his car.

The night manager tipped her chin up, eyed him down the length of her nose, then rattled his change across the counter and returned her attention to the television. Bruce waded back into the cold. He slicked the quarters into the phone and dialed direct. When the machine answered, he said, "Hey, it's me." He let a few seconds of tape spool out. "I've got Jane with me and we made it to Virginia." He paused, his breath misting on the air. "I told her all about you," he said. This was not true. He'd been afraid to mention Melinda to his daughter. "We're low on funds. I need you to Western Union us some cash, not too much, maybe a hundred bucks or so or whatever you can spare." He paused again, licked his lips. "Jane can't wait to meet you," he said. "The number at the hotel is—" His skin went prickly all over. "Well, shit," he said. He left the receiver dangling and hustled back to the office.

"What's the number here?" Bruce said.

He propped the door with his shoulder. A white cat darted outside between his legs. Without looking away from the TV, the night manager said, "You're letting the heat out."

Bruce stepped inside. The door inched shut on its hydraulic arm. The night manager laughed at something on TV.

"I need that number," Bruce said.

She held up her hand for quiet, waited a second for the commercial. Then, in a singsong voice, she recited the number and Bruce dashed back to the phone. The line was dead when he arrived. He pounded the receiver hard against the keypad until he felt his frustration waning. He hung up, rubbed his face with both hands. His breath came in ragged gasps. He repeated his daughter's name in his head—Jane, Jane, Jane, Jane—until he felt sufficiently composed. Then he walked back to the office, made certain the door was closed behind him, laid three bills on the desk, and asked politely for more change.

The night manager sighed. "You have a perfectly good phone in your room," she said. "You stood there and told me so yourself. If you want to call long distance, all we ask is that you leave a ten-dollar deposit. "

Bruce smiled and pushed his hands into his pockets and tried to look like somebody's father.

"Please," he said. "My little girl."

"What if those nice young men in 9 were to come around hunting money for the snack machine, and I'd given you all my change? How would that be? I'm not made of quarters."

"This is the last time," Bruce said.

The old woman pursed her lips and shook her head. The screen made a net of shadows on her face. Bruce worried she might refuse him, but, after a moment, she levered the register open, dredged up a handful of quarters, and counted them one by one into his palm. When he reached the phone, Bruce pinned the receiver between his shoulder and his ear, pushed all twelve coins into the slot. To his surprise, Melinda answered on the second ring. "Thank God," he said, his legs going flimsy with relief. "I've called a hundred times. Where you been?"

In a quiet voice, Melinda said, "Here."

Bruce took a moment to digest her answer.

"There?" he said.

"I'm sorry," Melinda said.

"I don't get it," he said.

"This is a bad idea," she said. "I mean—we hardly know each other, Bruce. I can't mother somebody else's little girl."

"We talked about it," he said. "You were excited."

"Now I've had a chance to think," Melinda said.

"Melinda," Bruce said. "Don't—"

"I'm sorry," Melinda said again. "I'm hanging up."

Then she did hang up and Bruce listened to the dial tone for a minute before placing the receiver in its cradle. Sixteen dimes dropped into the coin return. The cold seeped into his bones. Bruce slouched off to check on Jane. He refused to look at the night manager as he passed, but he did stop at the snack machine to blow seven of his dimes on a cheese Danish wrapped in plastic.

Jane was sprawled atop the blankets when Bruce returned, all awkward knees and elbows, as if she had fallen into bed from a tremendous height. She was four years old. She was wearing red corduroy overalls, a white turtleneck, and a blue quilted jacket. She was wearing sneakers and frilly socks. Until that morning, Bruce had never seen these clothes before. He cupped his hands and breathed into them to take the chill off. He palmed her brow. She was warm, a little clammy. She did not register his touch. Bruce tiptoed past and arranged himself on the second bed. He kicked his boots off and massaged the cold out of his feet. He emptied his pockets. Wallet, car keys, dimes. He had five cigarettes left in his pack. He had a small duffel in the bathroom. In it was a change of underwear, a pair of socks, a toothbrush, an electric razor, a stick of deodorant, and an unloaded .38 revolver. He thought he could convince Melinda to change her mind, but, if worst absolutely came to worst, he would find a pawn shop in the morning and sell the gun.

Bruce took off his jacket and propped his back against the headboard and watched ESPN with the sound off for a while. He ate the Danish. It tasted like newspaper. He eyed his daughter. She looked exactly like her mother. After a few minutes, he got up and went into the bathroom to smoke a cigarette. He didn't like to smoke around Jane. There was a louvered window in the shower and he cranked it open and wedged a towel under the door to block the draft. The window overlooked the Dumpsters in the alley behind the motel. He saw the white cat nosing around back there. He clucked his tongue and the cat looked at him like it had seen everything in the world. A man smoking in the john was nothing special.

He closed his eyes and tried to remember how it had been with Jane before his marriage ended, before Barbara met another man, before the judge let Barbara and her new husband take Jane up to New Jersey. He hadn't seen Jane in sixteen months and he wondered what she remembered, too, wondered how Barbara had portrayed him. He doubted he came off too well. Then he tried to figure what had spooked Melinda. He blamed her change of heart on a lack of imagination. He'd been gone a week and she needed him around to paint the picture, to hold her in his arms and whisper the future in her ear. Bruce opened his eyes. The cat was gone. He dragged on his cigarette, exhaled out the window. He couldn't tell where the smoke ended and his breath began.

When he was finished, Bruce flushed the cigarette and stood in the doorway watching his daughter sleep, her lips parted, her chest rising and falling in slow motion. He thought maybe he should get her out of those clothes and under the covers. There hadn't been time to pack Jane a bag and he wasn't sure which was better—undressed, no nightgown or fully clothed in bed. He tried to think what he might have done when he was still in practice. He decided to split the difference. He would take off her shoes and her jacket and her overalls but leave the turtleneck and socks. He crouched at the foot of her bed, unlaced her right shoe. As he was slipping it over her heel, Jane blinked and stretched her arms over her head.

"Daddy?" she said.

She gazed at Bruce, then at the shoe in his hand. He felt like he'd been caught in the act of stealing it from her.

"It's me," he said. "Remember, baby?"

He got her out of her shoes and took the jacket off and unfastened the overalls and pulled them over her legs. Jane let him do with her as he pleased. He scooped her up, his forearm beneath her thighs, and she hooked her feet behind his back. With his free hand, he turned the blankets down. Jane hid her face against his neck.

"I'm cold," she said. "Let's go to Mamma's house."

"I'll tell you what. We'll go to Mississippi instead. It never gets cold in Mississippi."

As he was getting her situated in bed, fluffing her pillow, organizing the blanket beneath her chin, she reached up and touched his cheek, an affectionate gesture, like he had said or done something to deserve it. She ran her finger over his lips, his eyebrow, the bridge of his nose.

"Will Mamma be in Miss-ssippi?" she said.

"You never know about your mamma," he said. "Your mamma's hard to read. You never know where your mamma might turn up."

But Jane had already drifted back to sleep. Bruce could hear a faint, congested burble in her lungs. He tucked the covers in around her, then walked over and checked the heating unit, passed his hand over the vent. He thought maybe Jane was right. The room was too cold for little girls. He could feel lukewarm air breathing out against his palm. He tried to turn it up, but the knob had been removed. He covered Jane's brow with one hand, his brow with the other. He wondered what, if any, restorative measures he should take. The only thing that occurred to him was aspirin, but he didn't have aspirin or know where to buy aspirin at one o'clock in the morning in an unfamiliar city or have enough money to buy aspirin with if he had known where to find it. He wasn't even sure if aspirin was safe for little girls.

"Jane," he said. "Jane, baby."

She lifted up on her elbows, her eyes groggy and uncertain, and, immediately, Bruce regretted waking her. Probably, all she needed was a little rest and here he was keeping her from it to ease his own concerns.

"Daddy?" she said.

"It's me," he said. "I'm sorry, sweetie. Go on back to sleep."

He held her shoulders and she let him push her back against the pillow. He stroked her hair for a minute. Then he said, "I'm sorry, baby, but, listen, while you're up, how 'bout tell me how you feel?"

"I'm cold," she said.

"Do you feel sick?" he said. "Do you feel like you have a fever?"

"It's cold in here," she said.

Jane curled herself into a fetal ball, her knees drawn up, her fists beneath her chin. Bruce pulled the covers to her neck. He didn't know exactly how to read her answer. It might mean chills, but it might not mean a thing. She had, after all, complained about the temperature before. He didn't want to give in to paranoia. He hadn't been responsible for anybody in a long time and he recognized the possibility that he was overreacting. It was true that Jane was warm to touch, but there was nothing so warm as a sleeping child. He remembered that. He sat on the edge of the bed and searched her face. She had changed immeasurably since he had seen her last. She was taller and she had gained some weight, of course, and her hair was cut in a style suitable for little girls, but there was something else, something that he couldn't put his finger on, as if all the things that she had seen in his absence and all the things she had come to know were apparent in her features.

When he was sure Jane was sleeping soundly, Bruce jotted the Saint John Divine's phone number on the back of his hand, filled his pocket with the leftover dimes, and walked outside to have another go at Melinda. The night manager didn't look away from the TV. It had started snowing while he was in the room. The flakes darted in the wind like schools of fish. He called collect, but Melinda didn't answer. Then he decided that collect was probably a bad idea—he needed to impress Melinda with his seriousness in this matter, with his paternal self-reliance—so he punched his last nine dimes into the slot. It rang twice before the operator interrupted to let him know he needed thirty-five cents to complete the call. Bruce hung up, listened to the rattle of his change. There were three quarters in the dispenser. He did the math, jiggled the tongue, no response. He stood there for a moment, the coins winking in his palm, his heart pounding in his chest, before starting for the office. He found the night manager exactly as he'd left her.

"I can't spare any more change," she said at his approach.

"That's what I want to talk about," Bruce said. "Your pay phone took my money."

She shook her head. "Not my problem. The phone is owned by an independent contractor. "

"It's on the side of your hotel," he said.

"You have to write a letter," she said. "That's how they do the refunds. The address is on the phone."

"I don't have time for that," he said. "I need to make this call tonight."

The night manager arched her right eyebrow.

"Is there a phone in your room?"

She looked at him a moment longer, then swung her gaze back to the TV. Bruce was determined not to be bullied. It was important, he thought, to raise a protest of some kind.

"The heater," he said. "It's freezing in our room and my little girl is sick. The knob is broken on the heating unit."

The night manager said, "We keep the wall units at sixty-eight degrees. The policy was spelled out on your registration form."

Bruce opened his mouth, but closed it without speaking. His muscles shook beneath his skin. He smacked the wire screen with the heel of his hand and the night manager flinched, then composed herself and settled her eyes on him again. In a steady voice, she said, "You don't want me to get the police." She reached for her phone and held the receiver up. The dial tone bleated at him like a taunt.

"Do you have kids?" he said, but the night manager didn't answer. She propped her feet on the counter and cradled the phone against her breast. A laugh track spilled from the TV.

Bruce walked outside without another word. He needed a minute to collect himself. He didn't want Jane to see him in this condition. The church was dark, regal in its silence. It wasn't an unappealing scene if you took the time to look around. Everything was quiet and the snow sparkled like the world was made of broken glass.

Just then, a man wearing a kimono over his clothes turned the corner and headed up the sidewalk in Bruce's direction. He made kissing noises as he walked. He smiled at Bruce and rubbed his arms and did a friendly shiver. Bruce nodded in reply.

"Have you by any chance seen a cat out here?" the man said. "A white cat. Fu Manchu whiskers." He drew imaginary whiskers in the air around his mouth.

"I saw him in the alley," Bruce said.

The man made a sad face. "I just came from there," he said. He covered his brow with his right hand. "I told Jerry we should have left him in the car. He would've been fine in the car, don't you think? Jerry said it was too cold, but look what's happened now."

"I'm sorry," Bruce said.

The man gave Bruce a meaningful shrug and shuffled down the sidewalk. Bruce thought of Jane sleeping in the room and felt suddenly alive and sure of himself, as if, after years of rotten luck, he had only to wait a short while longer before fortune smiled on him again. He hurried back inside and down the hall and worked his key into the lock. He opened the door to find his daughter's bed abandoned. He cast his gaze around the room in disbelief. His bed, her bed. The muted television. Her clothes still draped over a chair. The pillow held the imprint of her face. Then the toilet flushed and Jane emerged from the bathroom, looking pallid and exhausted.

"Dammit, Jane," he blurted. "You scared me half to death."

"I got sick," she said. "I'm sorry. I didn't mean—"

Her face contorted and she dissolved into blubbering. Bruce was disgusted with himself. He rushed over and picked her up and clutched her against his chest. Her body bucked with sobs.

"It's all right, Jane, baby. Daddy didn't mean to yell."

He carried her into the bathroom, surveyed the toilet. There were traces of vomit on the rim. The air smelled like spoiled milk. He shut the door, walked her in a circle, bouncing her lightly in his arms.

"I'm sorry, sweetie," he said. "You didn't do anything wrong. You did good. You made it to the bathroom and everything. Half the time, when Daddy's sick, he winds up hosing down the room."

"Mamma takes me to the potty when I'm sick," she said.

"Your mamma's an old pro," he said. "The potty is the place to be."

Jane was calming some. Bruce could feel her breath against his throat, the heat of her skin against his chest.

"Do you feel better?" he said.

Jane wagged her head. He couldn't tell if that meant yes or no. He carried her to the bed and laid her down.

"What else does Mamma do when you get sick?" he said.

Jane said, "I can't remember what she does."

"That's all right," he said. "We'll get it sorted out."

He ducked into the bathroom and returned with a wet rag. He wiped her face and neck and around her ears.

"How's that?" he said. "Is that good? Is that something Mamma would do?"

Jane nodded and sniffled.

"It'll be all right," Bruce said.

He waited until she was asleep before he crept into the bathroom for a smoke. He opened the window and gazed out at the night. While he watched, the white cat appeared from nowhere, leapt onto a stack of flattened cardboard boxes and peered in his direction. It looked bored and noble and indifferent to the snow. He thought of the women in his life—Barbara in New Jersey and Melinda in Mississippi and his daughter in the next room. They had loved him for a while. One day, he imagined, when the police had caught up to him and Jane had been returned safely to her mother, she might remember this night fondly, might at least look back with a measure of affection on the lengths to which her father had gone for their reunion. It wasn't impossible. He had heard of stranger things. Bruce fished the gun out of his duffel. He wanted to go another round with that night manager, revisit the issue of the phone. He didn't have any bullets, but he was feeling lucky just the same.

Killing Stonewall Jackson

Ghost Story won't tell you his real name. He's been shot fourteen times, still has lead in his kneecap and in the bones of his thighs and in two of his ribs. Pink scars pock his chest like extra nipples. There is a tumorous lump on his collarbone where he was nicked at Front Royal. He claims that he is thirty-four years old, but when he wakes this morning, coughing blood onto the back of his hand and limping around in dingy long johns, you'd swear he'd been alive a hundred years.

At Cedar Mountain, you see Eustace Wilson cut in half by a chain. The enemy has run out of artillery and is loading whatever they can find into the cannons—horse manure, broken-up slivers of wagon wheel. The chain makes a sound like a little boy whistling and takes Eustace apart just below his privates. His legs loll away to either side like a puppet's legs. His trunk thumps to the ground at your feet. His eyes are wide with surprise, his mouth gaping open and closed like he can't catch his breath. This is what they call the monkey show.

Ghost Story smokes tobacco rolled in corn husks. His best friend is a dwarf named Walpole. Walpole has a beard that drapes to his ankles, knotted with burrs and stained black around his mouth. When the army stops long enough, he makes whiskey from pine bark and lamp oil and rotted meat. He carries canteens of his concoction on the march instead of water. His hands and shoulders shake with palsy. His breath smells like kerosene.

The men tell stories about Stonewall Jackson. He keeps a colored whore and reads the Bible to her while she holds him in her mouth. He chews lemons even in the heat of battle. The day he earned his nickname he shot two dozen of his own men for attempting to flee the field. He sleeps standing like a horse. You see him up close one time, rounding a bend in the road with a group of officers, the horses dancing and blowing and bumping flanks. You are resting beside the road watching a hawk turn figure eights in the sky, and the general himself pulls up short and shouts *We are an army of the living God.* Then he spurs his mount, drawing the glittering officers in his wake, the horses giving rise to spirits of dust as they pass.

Every night Walpole breaks for the freedom of the woods and every night Ghost Story brings him back. Ghost Story waits until he thinks you are asleep, then glides over you in the tent, smelling vaguely of camphor and sweat. You can hear cicadas ringing in the trees and the droning of a thousand snores. If there's been a fight that day, you can hear the terrible voices from the field, the abandoned and speaking dead. Finally, Ghost Story's shadow reappears against the side of the tent and you close your eyes, pretending sleep, and listen to him nestling down beside you in the dark. Before he comes to bed, he lashes Walpole's beard to a tent post to keep him from escaping again. Each morning, his memory wiped clean by drink, Walpole is amazed anew to find himself unable to stand.

In a cornfield at Sharpsburg, you fight McClellan to a standstill. The crop is shaved to stubble, bodies lined up in rows exactly where they fell. There is a whitewashed church beside the field. The September leaves are just beginning to change. The men gather in the church before falling back and write their names on the wall: Gellar the Jew and Henry Cotton, Ugly Joe Noon and Watkins Price. Even little Walpole climbs on Ghost Story's shoulders and scratches his name above the rest. When he's finished, Ghost Story sets him down and pats his head. You watch Ghost Story as he runs his hands across the plaster, hoping he will add his name as well, but he says the wall looks like a tombstone to his eyes.

Winter brings stragglers to camp, country women and slaves with no place else to go. You are squatting in the woods, pouring your insides out, when this girl appears beside you like an apparition. She wrinkles her nose and says *Are you sick?* You smuggle hardtack from camp to feed her, take her down to the river, and pull her nightgown over her head and wash her hair in bone-cold water. Before the war, miners worked these rocks and panned this river for gold. The girl can't be more than twelve, thirteen years old. You watch the water running over her hands and bare ankles, the two of you wading in the shallows, looking for bits of gold the miners might have forgotten.

Gellar the Jew carries a bag of teeth for good luck. His father is a dentist. He has two long curls of coal-black hair dangling from beneath his infantry cap. Ugly Joe Noon writes letters and poems to a woman no one believes exists. On the march, you catalog the names Ghost Story has denied. At night, you dream Eustace Wilson playing cards. He's drinking Walpole's whiskey and winning all your money. His disembodied legs skitter from shadow to shadow just beyond the reach of the firelight. You wake screaming and Ghost Story smacks your head. He tells you shut your damnfool mouth.

You beat them back at Fredericksburg, hunkering in the sunken road, giving them canister and shot, watching their lines melt away like snow in the rain. It's so cold the wounded freeze before they bleed to death. The aurora borealis shows itself as far south as Black Mountain that night, the sky tracked red with streamers, running brighter than shooting stars. Watkins Price says that must be a good omen. Ghost Story says it's the just spirits of the dead hurrying from the field.

No one will share a tent with Walpole. He vomits black bile all the time. He is a belligerent drunk. His feet are blistered and rotten and even he can't stand the smell. At night, when Ghost Story brings him back to camp, he arranges Walpole's feet outside the tent, wipes them down with water from his canteen, and smears them with bacon grease. These are serious feet, big enough for a man twice Walpole's size. His toenails are yellow and hard as rail spikes. Ghost Story has to cut them down with his bayonet once or twice a week.

Sundays, now and then, General Jackson presides over the chapel service. He mounts the podium like he's going to ride it into battle and he is strictly Old Testament in his preaching. Henry Cotton, who is in charge of trimming the general's beard, says that God himself told Stonewall how to turn Nathaniel Banks at Port Republic. Jackson's beard is always well-groomed and shiny, edged at his chin with a dignified sprinkling of gray, his hair swept back beneath his hat with pomade. You see him some mornings turning his face side to side before a mirror, while Henry Cotton knots a gold sash around his waist.

The army is bivouacked near Zion Crossroads when the girl turns up again. It's evening, all fragile February light and wood smoke,

old songs and musty Bibles and letters home. You see her standing at the tree line, her nightgown breezing against her calves. You
bring her rice and she finds a worm as long as your finger in the
bowl. She says *We'll just eat acorns and live in the woods like squir-
rels.* When you ask if she is real, she laughs and slips out of her
nightgown and lies back on the brittle grass. You kneel between
her legs and take her in before nightfall—her pale hair spread like
a wing around her head, her boyish nipples, so skinny you can
count her ribs. You tell her that she's just a girl, this isn't what you
want. You close your mind to thoughts of other men in other camps
not so generous as you.

Ugly Joe Noon produces a letter from his woman at mail call. He
crouches by the fire and reads it out loud. I'll wait for you, Joe, the
letter says, no matter what happens. If you are killed in battle, the
letter says, I will keep myself pure until we meet again in Heaven.
The men fall quiet, loneliness settling over the morning like a fog.
Ugly Joe sifts through the pages again and again, as if he can hardly
believe what he's holding in his hands. The fire crackles and spits,
dark birds turn circles in the sky. Somewhere, way off, the orderly
patter of rifles. Then Gellar the Jew says *I'll bet his sister wrote it.*
All around the fire, men pick up the joke. Ugly Joe has his sister
writing him letters. Ugly Joe couldn't get a woman in a whorehouse.
Joe leaps to his feet, denies everything, takes a swing at Gellar the
Jew, but the men laugh even harder. After a while, he gives up trying to change their minds and consigns the pages to the fire.

Stonewall Jackson has blue eyes. He wears a bright yellow plume
in his hat and keeps ladies' underwear in his campaign chest, but
they turn up missing when a thief follows spring into camp. There
are new blooms and frightened grouse. Gellar the Jew loses a
pocket watch and one of his sidelocks is snipped from his head

while he sleeps. Watkins Price loses the brass buttons from his uniform. He has to tie his coat with strips of boot leather until he can scavenge a new one from a dead man. Henry Cotton loses a gold tooth. Briefly reinspired, Ugly Joe Noon swears that the thief has stolen the rest of his beautiful love letters. Ghost Story sleeps with his bayonet even though he has nothing to lose. From his map table, General Jackson scrawls out a bounty: twenty Confederate dollars for the identity of the brigand.

One night you hear voices from Walpole's tent. He and Ghost Story are just back from their nightly cat-and-mouse. You sit in the darkness and eavesdrop. There's Walpole mumbling like his mouth is full of mud. You've never heard him speak a single coherent word but Ghost Story understands him. He says *That's right. We'll be up to our armpits in island girls. Hell, you'll be over your head. They'll have round bellies and skin as brown as baseball gloves. Just let me get your beard tied. There now. That's right. You sleep now, Walpole.* For a long time after he returns to the tent, he shifts his legs, trying to get comfortable against the ground. The white canvas glows in the moonlight like you are bedded down inside a Chinese lantern. Finally, when you can't stand the quiet anymore, you ask Ghost Story if he has ever been in love. After a moment, he says *Yes* and that is all. The wind pushes leaves against the tent. You open the flap and look out at the night, all the sleeping men, death close upon them in their dreams. You can hear horses snuffing and tugging at the grass, the faint ticking of armaments like silverware on a dinner plate. Then you say *Tell me your name, Ghost Story. Someone should know your name in case something happens.* He rolls over so the two of you are back to back. Softly, he says *The army knows my name.*

Ugly Joe Noon is killed in a skirmish at Kelly's Ford. Gellar the Jew salvages his pack and searches it for evidence of the mystery woman. He finds a tattered daguerreotype of a girl with the same sloping forehead and crooked teeth as Ugly Joe, the same harelip and weak chin and shovel nose. He shows you the picture and says *Has to be his sister, don't you think? No way Ugly Joe had a woman.* He takes the picture from your hands, folds it carefully, and hides it in the leather pouch with all his lucky teeth.

The girl finds you on sentry duty. The woods are dark, crazy with insect chatter, and you don't hear her slipping up behind you, running her arms around your waist. She tells you it's fine that there is no food tonight. She came here to see you. She eases you back against a warm flat rock and pushes herself down over you, her hair swinging at her cheeks. When you protest, she covers your mouth with her hand. You tell her this means she'll have to marry you when the war is over. You tell her that you want to meet her family, and she says they're all dead, mother and father, four brothers and eight sisters. When you close your eyes, you see Ghost Story chasing Walpole through the woods, his breath huffing in and out, his eyes bright in the moonlight, his stride cantered and smooth like some nameless animal. You want to tell the girl to stop, but it's too late for that.

You dream Ugly Joe Noon dancing with his sister, Eustace Wilson reunited with his legs. Walpole is eleven feet tall, his eyes clear, his hair neatly combed and dyed with bootblack. Ghost Story is bathing in a swiftly running river, shedding scars and tumors like snakeskins, and you wish you could find a place for yourself in this dream of restoration.

Sometimes, Walpole trips over his beard. Ghost Story breaks rank and hauls him up by the collar, carries him under his arm until the order comes to halt. The line bumps to a stop, like rail cars. His beard is too thick to be cut by scissors or knives so, after dinner, Ghost Story holds Walpole over the fire by his ankles, lets the hair catch and burn a few inches toward his face, then pinches it out with his fingers. Walpole blusters and fights, twists his body like a snake, but Ghost Story refuses to let him go. Moths flicker in the firelight. Ghost Story keeps burning it back until Walpole stinks like poison and the beard is nothing more than a singed goatee. He scrubs his face with whiskey and water, runs a wire brush under his fingernails, dunks his head in a pot of scalding water. When he's finished, Walpole shimmers pinkly in the darkness, glowing like a new June bride.

The thief returns before Easter. Gellar the Jew loses his boots and his second curl. Henry Cotton loses twenty-seven pounds to dysentery. Watkins Price loses his right eye when his rifle backfires on the parade ground. And you begin to lose your memory of the girl. It's been a month since her last appearance and somehow you know you're not going to see her again. You try to think of her at night so she won't slip away completely, how you groped along the bottom of the creek and warmed her cold fingers in your mouth, how you fed each other acorns like grapes and whispered promises against her neck. Walpole sees you moping and offers you a swig from his canteen.

These days, Walpole's beard is too short to lash him to the post, so Ghost Story is up and down all night. He asks do you mind if he sleeps nearest the tent flap. You listen to him slipping into the night and listen when he returns. He ties Walpole with strips of bedding, but Walpole gnaws through the cloth with his rotten teeth. Once he tries bringing Walpole into the tent with the two of you, but he farts and grumbles like he's speaking backward and eventually Ghost Story picks him up by the belt and pitches him out-side. *You're on your own, jackass,* he says. But when Walpole has had a chance to go scurrying away, his footsteps tiny, almost sound-less on the grass, Ghost Story lumbers painfully to his feet and is on the trail again. Finally, after nearly two weeks, Ghost Story returns alone. He drops at the mouth of the tent, lights a husk of rolled tobacco without lifting his head. *I'm too tired,* he says, his voice blue smoke. In the distance is the deep bass note of cannon fire. You say *I never figured why you didn't just let him go before.* Ghost Story sighs, drapes an arm across his face. He says *Walpole won't last a minute on his own.* You say *Maybe he'll surprise you* and he says *Yes, that's right, maybe he will.*

Letters mark the days that you have lived. You write to the girl, but you tear the letters up before they are finished, not only be-cause you have no place to send them, but because the right words, all full of reverence and apology, are impossible to say. Gellar the Jew writes to Joe's sister, tells her that Ugly Joe was brave and honest and talked about her all the time. His last words were of his dear sister, Gellar writes, though you were there and you know this not to be the case. The sister writes back and Gellar writes again and so on. In the evening, with all the sad harmonicas blow-ing, Gellar the Jew unfolds her picture and holds it to the setting sun. He says *She's not so ugly. Do you think?* You give him an eye-brow raise, and he says *No really. Look. You just have to see her in the right light.* He holds the picture up again and tilts it back and forth. *Look here,* he says, *Look here.*

Nine men are shot for desertion on nine successive days, lashed to a wagon wheel and made heavier with lead. Each time the bugle calls you to formation, Ghost Story's face goes pale. You hurry to the parade ground, form up and watch General Jackson lift his hat above his head, then let it drop, a lemon wedge clutched between his teeth, but the dead man is never Walpole. Stonewall watches without emotion, slips a hand under his coat and adjusts the wire on his corset. The air is rich with echoes. Sometimes, Ghost Story creeps outside at night and vanishes for hours. But more often than not, he lies beside you and fails at sleeping, his limp growing more pronounced every day, his back bending into a stoop, all the old wounds refusing to let him rest.

You dream Walpole chasing island girls across packed sand, his feet jeweled with salt water, his beard flying over his shoulder like a cape. He offers them gifts to ply their legs apart, a matching pair of sidelocks and a gold tooth, brass buttons and your memory of the girl. Walpole must have ten children in the dream, each of them hobbling around on their father's stubby legs, calling out to him with unpronounceable words.

When you have marched fourteen miles in an afternoon and routed the enemy at Chancellorsville, General Jackson rides out along the front to survey his position. The wounded are pleading on the field because someone didn't do a proper job of killing. Ghost Story has been sent to the picket line without supper. Gellar the Jew starts another letter to Joe's sister. He says *Would you read this for me? I've never been very good at saying things right.* Just as he is handing over the pages, you hear the report of a single rifle, and six days later old Stonewall is dead, his amputated arm buried in a separate grave. *We were scared,* Ghost Story says, *Someone must have mistaken him for the enemy.* He winks and roots around in his pack, comes out with a canteen of whiskey that you didn't know he'd saved. He gets himself drunk enough to sleep. *Popskull,* he says, raising his tin cup, *O Be Joyful.*

Sometimes, when new prisoners have been taken, you ask them if they've seen a girl in the woods. *She's always hungry,* you say, *I knew her a long time ago.* They have haircuts, these men, and their uniforms are clean. They are happy to be done with fighting. They cross their boots at the ankle and link their fingers behind their heads and say that if they had found a girl in the woods the army wouldn't have seemed so bad.

Watkins Price sees Stonewall with his blind eye. Henry Cotton hears him in his sleep. They talk strategy and women's clothes. He saves the hair from General Jackson's comb, sprinkles it in the furrows of a tobacco field, hoping that Stonewall will sprout from the ground with the summer crop. Gellar the Jew believes that Stonewall is still alive, that he's been sent west in secret to remedy the situation along the Mississippi. Once, you catch Ghost Story humming while he shaves, his jawbone lathered with soap. You ask him why he's so pleased, and he tells you that the days are growing longer now.

The army moves north without Stonewall, as though nothing has changed, through Maryland and Pennsylvania, then back across the Rappahannock toward home. You run through names for Ghost Story to pass the time. Saul, Jacob, Daniel, John. You have an idea that you won't be allowed many more guesses before he puts an end to the discussion altogether. So you study him quietly, trying to match a name to his features. There is a burn scar on his cheek shaped like a thumb, a lint bandage on his neck where he was grazed at Little Round Top. Gellar the Jew weighs in with Edgar. Henry Cotton thinks it's Richard, and you have to agree there is a Richardly curve to his broken nose. But Ghost Story shakes his head when you suggest that particular name. You are digging graves, the worst duty in the army, and he stops for a second to wipe the sweat from his brow. He rests a heel on the butt of his shovel. Crows are hopping on the new mounds, dawn skimming on the bottoms of the clouds. Ghost Story mutters to himself, a string of words that you don't understand, then shades his eyes and lets his gaze wander, as always, to the shadowy woods.

The End of Everything

Then there's the one about the woman who comes home from work and discovers her dog—sometimes a Doberman, sometimes a Lab—gasping and gagging and giving her walleyed looks from the phony oriental rug in the foyer. The woman is generally a secretary or a dental hygienist, depending on who is telling the story, but she pitches the dog over her shoulder, like she has been rehearsing for this moment all her life, carries him to the car, and is doing an obstacle course run through the tag end of rush hour on the way to the emergency veterinary clinic. She loves her dog. She picked him up at the pound eight weeks after her divorce, and they have grown to rely on each other in a very real way. She skids sideways into the parking lot, bangs the double doors open like a TV paramedic, and starts barking orders and detailing her situation and letting an old lady with an asthmatic parakeet know that she is going to have to wait. The vet has seen her like this before—when the dog was bitten by a garden snake, when the dog was kicked in his ribs for snapping at the paperboy—and he speaks to her in soothing tones, exactly the same way he will speak to her dog in a few minutes. He explains how everything is going to be all right, there appears to be some sort of obstruction in her dog's throat, but the fact that he can get air in his lungs—never mind the wheezing and convulsing—is definitely a good sign.

"My assistant is already administering a sedative." He pats her shoulder in an infuriating, patronizing way. "I know you're worried. But no conscious dog in the world will let you put forceps down his throat."

He hitches his belt, goes on to say that it will be a few hours before they know anything, an hour or two more before the dog comes around. She might as well go on home until they call. She protests at first but after securing a promise that her dog will be his number one priority, she lets the vet convince her to leave.

The house is quiet when she returns. Despite everything, she is saddened and suddenly wasted with exhaustion when there is no dog to greet her at the door. She feels her way down a dark hallway to the kitchen, retrieves a bottle of gin from the freezer, a paper cup from the pantry, and carries them, along with the portable phone, into the living room. She slumps onto the couch, swinging her knees open like a man. When she closes her eyes, she can see yawning, cavity-filled mouths—make her a dental hygienist—and hear the electric whine of the drill and smell whitener and the sulfur smell of ground enamel. She remembers, then, how she got her dog. She was down at the Movie Merchant, browsing for a romantic comedy, when a man walked in with his son, the boy crying and lugging a black Lab puppy under his arm. She asked the boy why he was so upset, and he said his daddy couldn't afford two dogs. They'd had to leave the last of the litter at the pound. She felt seasick the rest of the evening, had nightmares in her sleep. She has always had a weakness for lost causes and strays. Now, she sips gin, takes a measure of comfort in her distress. It has been a long time since she was this devoted to another living thing.

When the phone rings, she is almost asleep. She comes to in a hurry and fumbles for the receiver and hears her vet shouting, "Get out of your house, lady! This is no joke. I already called the police."

She checks her watch; only a few minutes have passed. Her mind is cottony with fatigue.

"Is the dog all right?"

"Never mind the dog," he says. "The dog is fine. I'm telling you we found a human finger in his throat. There's somebody in your house, hear? You gotta get out *now*."

She drops the phone without hanging up, understanding washing over her, and whips her head around looking for the intruder. The house is dim and full of shadows. Her heart is a drumroll all of a sudden, her spine a column of glass. The vet's voice is still buzzing from the phone, distant and frenzied and too small to understand. Her reflection in the window sends her backward over the coffee table, but she regains her feet and is running hard for the kitchen, dodging shadows and waving her arms. She finds her purse, snatches a taser from among the gum wrappers and lipsticks and dog biscuits and heads for the door, holding the stun gun out in front of her like a compass, then out into the yard and she's spinning on the grass, window lights whirling around her, not knowing which way to escape first.

The story, as it is usually told, ends here. The woman is left hanging somewhere between safety and certain death. In this particular version, however, it occurs to her that it has been more than an hour since she found the dog and she wonders, even in the midst of panic, what sort of burglar or rapist or serial killer would lose a finger to a dog and still linger at the scene of his intended crime. She slows herself down, stops spinning and scans the house, door left open in flight, parted curtains in the bedroom, faint light from the kitchen, everything more or less normal. She pushes the hair out of her eyes and waits for her wind to come back. She wants to get this sorted out. The police are on their way. The intruder is just as likely hiding outside as in the house, just as likely gone. Slowly, warily, she creeps back up the steps and through the front door, lighting the house as she goes, through the dining room safely and into the kitchen, through the living room, the discarded phone still on the floor, an operator's voice bleating tonelessly out, then down the long hall headed for the bedroom. A heady calm comes over her as she walks, as if the course of this night was decided long ago, such an overwhelming relief that she doesn't see the faint brown drops of blood on the carpet beneath her feet, doesn't stop to check the bathroom sink, doesn't even notice, as she stands in the bedroom with one hand on the light switch, the other clutching the stun gun, that the closet door is swinging soundlessly open behind her.

A chill hand drops on her shoulder and she spins, leading with the taser, and sends her ex-husband hurtling back into the closet. There is a moment, just before he brings her dresses and shelves avalanching down on top of him, when he is suspended in midair and she recognizes his face, his mouth frozen in a beautiful rictus of pain and surprise. Then he's in among the shoes and belts, buried under a landslide of listless scarves and neatly pressed hygienist uniforms and jazzy blouses she never wears. A solitary leg extends from beneath the wreckage, his tennis shoe dappled with dried paint. Her ex is a painter of houses. She shocks him once more on the ankle for scaring her before digging him out. When he stops convulsing enough to stand, she helps him up and sits him on the bed, his feet dancing on the carpet in a rhythm of fading currents. His right hand is a giant Q-Tip, all bloody beach towel and toilet paper and masking tape.

"Jimmy," she says, punching him in the chest. "I thought you were Son of goddamn Sam in my closet."

"You shocked me," he says. "F-f-f-fuck."

His eyes are glazed, his cheeks spasming all over his face. She can smell alcohol on his breath and in his clothes.

"I ought to pop you again," she says. "What are you doing here, Jimmy? Why on earth were you hiding in my closet?"

Jimmy holds up his Q-Tip hand, says, "Your dog bit my damn f-f-finger off."

She draws a breath and closes her eyes. The cadence of this conversation is as familiar as the sound of her dog breathing beside the bed at night. Her questions, his answers, six and a half years of talking at cross-purposes. She exhales slowly, rubs circles on her temple with two fingers. He is looking at her with a contrite face, those handsome, hangdog eyes.

"What I mean, Jimmy, is why were you here in the first place?"

She keeps herself calm, wills her heart to beat slowly. The hardest thing she has done in her whole life is rid herself of anger.

"Dorothy left me," Jimmy says. "I thought maybe you and I could—"

She shocks him again and leaves him flopping around on the bed, while she pops into the bathroom to check her hair. She's a mess but hasn't time to fix it now. While she's there, she rinses Jimmy's blood from the sink, wonders how often she's cleaned up after him over the years, remembers, then, that the police will be arriving soon. She imagines forms to fill out, charges to press or not. The fact is she doesn't feel up to it tonight. Back in the bedroom, Jimmy is face down on the floor, his arms straight out like a t. She rolls him over and he says, "Stop shocking me. Please, baby. I got a broken heart."

"Me too," she says. "C'mon, shitheel." She hauls him up, drapes his arm over her shoulder. "We need to clear out. Let's get you to a hospital."

Stories of this nature are obliged to generate a certain amount of pulse-increasing, campfire-style suspense. As a result, romantic history—all infidelity and forgiveness, infidelity and forgiveness— is less important, say, than the fact that the highway is suddenly empty of cars and the moon is ripe and the whole night is gauzed in nebulous mist.

"I can't go to the hospital," Jimmy says.

His leg jerks like a reflex test, and he steadies it with his good hand.

"You lost a finger," she says.

"Not the whole thing."

She pulls the car onto the shoulder and gets the interior light going. Jimmy is clutching his injured hand against his chest. When she tries to take a closer look, he turns his back and hunches over the pain. But she has seen enough. The wrapping is soaked all the way through and heavy with blood. She holds his chin in her hand and forces him to face her. His skin is sallow, his cheekbones high and pale, his hair damp with sweat and drooping down over his eyes. Jimmy has always been petrified by doctors.

"Why were you in my closet?"

"I was looking for more towels," Jimmy says. "I musta passed out."

She raises her eyebrows and nods so he'll understand. "And you think your stump-ass finger is just gonna scab up. Get a good night's sleep and you'll be fine in the morning. Look at yourself. Your hand is big as a medicine ball."

Jimmy lowers his eyes, dabs his face with the flannel tail of his shirt. He gives her a shy, woozy smile and says, "You look great, baby. You haven't gotten fat or anything."

"Don't start," she says. "You only have nine fingers."

Despite her jangled nerves, she can feel a blush surfacing in her cheeks. Jimmy inches toward her on the upholstery, pokes her hip with his good hand.

"Your hair's cut," he says. "I see you got your teeth fixed."

"They do it free for employees," she says.

"I still love you," he says.

She studies him for a long moment, crickets sawing frantically in the silence between them, the catalog of his betrayals rising in her throat. Jimmy winks, and she clamps down on his bandage with both hands. He throws his head back and howls, his lovely face wrenched tight with pain. She reaches across him, opens the door, and kicks him out onto the shoulder. He wails and rolls around on his back like an insect, his hand curled against his stomach. Then she jerks the car into drive and mashes down on the accelerator, the door thumping shut with her momentum, a spume of gravel in her wake.

Mile markers snap past, street lights taper off in the rearview mirror. The window is down, her hair dancing around her face. She feels so good she doesn't start worrying about Jimmy for almost fifteen minutes. She remembers the last time she took him to the hospital. She found him in their bed, busy with another woman, and she crept up and clubbed him with an iron. He slumped unconscious and the woman fled naked from the house. For a long time, she sat beside him, his hair oily with blood, his breathing peaceful as sleep. Now, she thinks of her dog, breathless and crazy-eyed with panic, thinks of Jimmy bleeding his life away beside the road. She knocks the steering wheel with the heel of her hand, bumps across the median, and heads back the other way.

Past a row of lit billboards she goes, past a wall of lightless trees, the history of her marriage playing in her mind as familiar and hackneyed as a Sunday movie. She recalls, not the endless series of deceptions and confessions, not the sound of a door opened in the middle of the night so as not to be heard, not his footsteps on the carpet while she pretended sleep, not even the smell of other women on his hands and in his hair when he came to bed unwashed. She recalls instead the hours before, when she would empty his dinner into the disposal and watch TV until it was so late she could no longer pretend she wasn't waiting up. Then the dark and the quiet and the empty bed. That was the worst of all. But the bitterness she wanted to feel over being left alone wasn't available to her—after all, men have been leaving women behind in stories since the beginning of language—so she settled for the threadbare anger of her betrayal. She could have forgiven him the women. She felt a strange comfort, in fact, the night she found him in her bed with someone else, was swamped with pity at the sight of him broken against the pillows. It was the hollowness of an empty house that stayed with her. And, while she hadn't realized it at the time, he had returned her to that feeling tonight, when she was waiting to hear about the dog, and it fills her a second time when she reaches the stretch of road where she stranded him and finds him gone.

She coasts along and scans the ditch. The gravel is scuffed where she left him flailing. The trees across the ditch are poker-faced. She is instantly afraid. She drives a few feet and stops, rakes her hands through her hair, idles over a rise in the highway and spots him in the near distance, weaving crookedly along the shoulder, his hand cradled against his stomach. She eases up beside him, cranks the window down to coax him into the car. When she's close enough, she can hear that he is singing an Eagles song.

"I won't let you take me to a doctor," he says, without looking at her. "Those doctors killed Mother Curtis."

"Your grandmother had cancer, Jimmy." Relief sifts over her. This, too, is an argument they have had before. "Your grandmother smoked four packs of Lucky Strikes a day."

"She didn't have the cancer until she got to the hospital," he says.

She sighs and leans toward him across the seat. "If you don't let me take you, you're gonna bleed to death."

"I got nothing to live for," he says. He covers his eyes with his good hand, but she knows he is watching her between his fingers. "Dorothy's gone and my wife doesn't love me anymore."

"Ex-wife, Jimmy," she says. "Remember the lawyers?"

"Let's just get one drink." He holds up his Q-Tip hand, looks at it for a moment, eyes confused, then drops it to his side and lifts the good hand to show her his index finger. "Just one. A little courage before the hospital."

He staggers, falls against the hood, rights himself and falls again, sitting down hard in the gravel. That was real, she thinks. He brings his arms up to circle his knees, studies the ground like he's surprised to find it there. She stops the car and pushes his door open.

"All right, Jimmy," she says. "I don't have money for a bar, but I know a place where we can go."

"You won't take me straight to a hospital?"

"Have I ever lied to you before?"

He mulls it over for a few seconds, picks up a piece of gravel and flicks it into the road. She puts the car in park and slides across the seat, climbs out and stands over him, offering her hand to help him up. He places his hand in hers but makes no move to stand.

"When did you get a dog?" he says.

She rubs the backs of his fingers with her thumb. Jimmy glances up at her, his face smooth, his eyes wide and melancholy and surprised, like she has just announced that she is getting re-married and he's been hoping all this time they might have another go at love. She says, "I got a dog when I heard they wouldn't fuck you over every time the wind blew funny."

"That's me, I guess?" he says. She knows he wants her to tell him otherwise, wants her to say she understands he is a good man in his heart, wants her to say she forgives him, but she won't tell him that.

In a sad voice, he says, "It's true. You never lied to me in all your life."

The last scene has to move with all the terrifying certainty of the beginning, has to be filled with an equivalent amount of menacing detail—dark birds backdropped by a yellow moon, ragged clouds sweeping across the night—while heightening whatever emotional tension, however tangential, has been established up to this point. Something along these lines: When Jimmy is belted into his seat, our heroine drives back down the highway to the office where she works. A glad-eyed neon incisor hovers over the parking lot, wearing a top hat and carrying a cane. The dentist has her lock up some nights, open mornings, so she has a key.

She helps Jimmy from the car, lets him lean against her, and leads him past the receptionist's desk to an examination room in back. He sprawls in the patient's chair, knocking the stainless steel instrument tray aside with his shoulder. She lifts his heels onto the footrest.

"I'm cold," he says.

She stands on a pedal in the floor and lowers him into a reclining position. "You're the one didn't want to go to a hospital."

She wheels the nitrous oxide cylinder over to the chair, gives the knob a full crank, and holds the mask over her own mouth to be sure the gas is flowing properly. Four deep breaths and her peripheral vision goes soft. "Here," she says, strapping the mask over his nose and mouth. "This won't take long. Two minutes and you'll be brave enough for a hundred hospitals."

She leaves him drawing gas and slips back to the front of the building to make sure the coast is clear. Theirs is still the only car in the lot. The neon incisor flickers and catches, flickers and catches. The wind floats a Styrofoam cup like something from a magic show. She tells herself to stop worrying about Jimmy, digs the cellular from her purse, dials the emergency clinic and when the vet answers, she says, "How's my good, brave dog?"

"Is everything all right?" he says. He sounds genuinely relieved to hear her voice. "The police called. They said nobody was home."

"It's a long story," she says. "Right now, I'm just thinking about my dog."

"Are you drunk? You sound funny."

"The dog?" she says.

"Should be waking up any minute," he says. "You can pick him up whenever. But I wouldn't feed him until morning. Sometimes, with the anesthesia and everything, they get a little queasy."

She pins the phone against her shoulder, flips through a worn issue of *People* magazine. She says, "Thank you for warning me before. You're a good man, doctor."

"It's Oscar," he says. The line is quiet a moment, then he adds, "I don't mean to be too aggressive, but I'm finished here at midnight. You wouldn't feel like a cup of coffee or anything?"

She thumbs a few pages, lingers on a photographic essay about a film festival out west somewhere, movie stars in ski suits posing on the slopes, cozy models in fur hats smoking cigarettes beside a fire. There are wilted flowers at the sign-in station. The other hygienist is a newlywed. She can hear the vet breathing into the phone, a clock ticking. Jimmy's voice, blurred by the mask and an octave high, comes to her from the other room. "Welcome to the Hotel California," he is singing, "such a lovely place, such a lovely place."

She says, "You ever have to put a dog to sleep?"

"Your dog doesn't need to be put down," he says. "Like I told you, you can pick him up whenever."

"I know," she says, "I was just thinking he's going to die one day. It makes my stomach hurt."

"Comes with the shorter life span." His voice is suddenly heavy with veterinary woes. "You always know you're going to outlive your pet. Unless you have a tortoise or something, but you don't see many of those around here. Look, maybe we should do coffee when you're feeling more lively."

"That's probably best," she says and hangs up. For a few minutes, she stares out the window, the magazine open on her lap. Streetlamps pick up the glitter of mica in the asphalt. The storefronts across the street are dark.

Jimmy is all smiles when she returns. His good hand propped behind his head, his feet crossed at the ankles. His breath fogging the see-through mask.

"Hey, baby," he says, infinitely glad to see her, "you remember that time we went fishing up in Dickinson County and you thought you got bit by a snake?"

"You're not stuttering your F-words," she says.

"My speech is fffffully lubricated," he says, drawing out the F to prove his point. He scoots over, pats the space for her to sit. "Don't you remember? You left the boat to take a leak, and a bee or a sticker or something got you. You thought a snake had bit you on the ass."

"I remember," she says, brushing the hair out of his eyes. "I also remember you sucking on my butt for a long time before you told me there wasn't any poison back there."

"That ain't all," he says, chuckling behind the mask.

"Gimme some of that."

He hands her the mask and she inhales and exhales, the gas candy-smelling and cold. Her ears fill with the sound of rushing water. She can feel a loosening in the backs of her legs. Jimmy has gone so white she can see blue traces of vein at his temples. His chest is soaked with blood where he is resting his hand against his ribs. His eyes are glazed with a watery film.

"We need to get you to the hospital," she says.

"Not yet, baby," he says. "Sit by me for a while."

She re-situates the mask over his face and curls up beside him, lays her head on his shoulder, wonders how long it has been since he lost his finger. Three hours, maybe four. He is rank with sweat, but the smell is somehow comforting and familiar. She says, "Why'd she leave you, Jimmy?"

He coughs and shifts his shoulder beneath her head.

"I couldn't quit talking about you, baby," he says. "I went on and on. I couldn't quit with the times we had."

"That's not true," she says.

He says, "You don't know everything."

She can sense him leaning forward, and, after a moment's hesitation, she lifts her chin to receive his kiss, bumps her nose against the plastic, and they laugh. She removes his mask and kisses him again, a lingering kiss, his lips icy against hers, his plump tongue heavy in her mouth.

"We were good together," he says, his voice coagulated and dull. "You should have never let me go."

"That's right, Jimmy," she says. The walls are lined with posters, gum disease and tooth decay and root canal charts. There is a giant molar flossing itself and a dozen brushes in a chorus line. They are singing a song—*Brushing three times a day keeps the cavities away*—and kicking their slender toothbrush legs. She undoes the top three buttons of Jimmy's shirt and moves her head to his chest, listens until she can hear his heartbeat, a barely discernible tremor beneath his skin. She remembers this rhythm, too, rolls her ear against his ribs to hear it better, tucks her fingertips into the waistband of his jeans. She wonders if she has been killing him all along. She loves him, even if she wished him dead a thousand ways every time he left before, even if she once swallowed a bottle of sleeping pills and retched them up before they did the job. Now, as if Jimmy is reading her mind, brown liquid fills the mask, dribbles down his chin, over his neck. She stands and removes the mask and rolls him on his side. He vomits again and she is filled with such an abiding sympathy she can hardly keep her feet. She has always loved him most when he was most in need. Jimmy looks at her from the tops of his eyes and she thinks that she could go on loving him forever if he was dying all the time. He slumps in the chair, his arms dangling over the side, a viscous thread of blood seeping from his bandage. All at once she is weak with fear. She begs Jimmy to stand. She lifts him by the armpits, and helps him up, but his knees give out and he carries her to the floor. She is crying, dragging him down the hall by his wrists, pleading with him, but he doesn't answer. There is no strength in her arms. She sits beside him, waits to catch her breath, assures herself that all she has to do is get him outside. Fifty feet is all and out the door and ten yards to the car. The hospital is just a few minutes away. Then she's doing it, hauling him across the asphalt and buckling the seat belt at his hip. His head hangs forward on his neck, lolls side to side when she takes a curve, his eyes sunken and black with shadow. But the road is clear for miles and every light is green. "Would she do this, Jimmy?" she says, her words swept away by rushing wind. "Would she love you half to death?" And she knows that, in a story like this one, the end of everything is always at your heels.

The Mesmerist

Moody boarded The Silver Star bound for DC, where he would hop The Crescent and ride it through the night. There was a dinner theater in New Orleans looking for a mesmerist to open the show and he had played well there in the past. In the seat opposite his, a girl was reading a fashion magazine. She was wearing a sweatshirt (Boston University Chamber Music Society), and every few seconds she tucked the same wayward strand of hair behind her ear. Moody had a gift for reading people and, in this girl, he recognized a sadness, something familiar and close to his heart. He saw it in the slump of her shoulders. He saw it in the hint of wear and tear around her eyes. She was hopeful and afraid. She had been unlucky all her life. This girl would have a broken heart before too long.

"Are you watching me?" she said. "I hate being watched."

She closed the magazine and leveled a glare at Moody. In one motion, he reached into the pocket of his coat, withdrew a penlight, and flicked the beam across her line of sight. He said, "Every muscle in your body is limp now. I am pulling your eyes closed with silken threads." The girl opened her mouth, but instead of speaking, she slumped in her seat. He counted down from ten to one and when he was finished, she was perfectly asleep. Her hands upturned and pendulous beside her. Her head bobbing as they rocked across a trestle. She looked vaguely surprised.

In Philadelphia, Moody steered her along in the tide of exiting passengers. He bought a pair of tickets in a sleeping berth to Cleveland. While they rolled cross-country in the dark, Moody described the life they would have together. He said she would never be lonely. He told her she would be possessed of grace and charm. He rambled until morning. "I'm going to count again," he said. "This time, when you wake, you will no longer be acquainted with unhappiness."

Moody found day work and they rented in a neighborhood sumptuous with brick and shade. They were happy for a while. Penelope took piano lessons from an elderly woman on the block, Mrs. Berryman, who often stopped Moody on the street and said, "That Penelope of yours is the most confident beginner I've ever had. It's like she knows piano in her bones." If the weather was right for open windows, Moody could hear her practicing when he walked home at night. He would stand in the yard marveling at the simple bricks and elegant maples and surprise himself with the notion that this was the life he had been looking for all his days.

One evening, already within earshot of Penelope's piano, Moody spotted a stranger peeking in the windows. It was fall, leaves chameleoning on their branches. Moody hurried up the street, called a friendly hello, wondered aloud what the man was doing on his porch. The man smiled in what Moody guessed was meant to be a reassuring way.

"I'm a private investigator," he said. "I've been looking for a girl." He retrieved a photograph from his briefcase—Penelope with a green ribbon pinned to her shoulder.

"What did she win?" Moody said.

"Second prize in the Fairfax County Piano Recital," he said. "She did Chopin. Her name's Penelope."

Moody slipped his penlight from his pocket, flicked the beam in his practiced manner. He lowered his voice and said, "You have made a mistake. There is no Penelope here."

"I have made a mistake," the man repeated. "There is no Penelope here."

His eyes were glazed, his mouth hanging open. The photograph fluttered from his fingertips.

Moody said, "Perhaps she has run off to Honduras. You should go down and have a look."

"Perhaps she has run off to Honduras," the man said. "I should go down and have a look."

Moody watched him stagger up the sidewalk to his car and drive away. He bent and picked up the picture, stood looking at it until Penelope's music came back to him, a melancholy sound on the fragile air.

At Christmas, they invited lonely Mrs. Berryman over and after dinner she sat beside Penelope on the piano bench and they played duets of holiday songs. When she was tired, they bundled Mrs. Berryman into her coat and walked her home. They stood at the curb and watched the snow gathering on the hood of Moody's car.

Penelope said, "I love how the snow muffles and magnifies everything at the same time. My voice sounds so loud just now."

Moody slipped his arm around her waist, let the deepening silence drift back in behind her words. He kissed the top of Penelope's head, her hair cold and brittle and dusted with snow.

He said, "You should have worn your hat."

"I'll be fine," she said. "You mother me too much, Moody."

She leaned her head on his shoulder and drew him against her. Christmas trees shone through parted curtains. The snow sparkled. Moody wondered if their footprints would be covered by morning.

Keeper of Secrets, Teller of Lies

Except for a desk clerk in a black beret, an old man with a fishhook in his thumb, and a woman and her young son, both of whom were periodically doubled over by violent, booming coughs, Dennis Hill had the emergency room to himself. This was Tuesday, half past noon, November 17. The little boy had been making faces at Dennis for twenty minutes. Now, he gaffed the corners of his mouth, stretched his lips apart as far as they would go. He folded his eyelids and rolled his pupils back into his head. By way of reply, Dennis did his best, most flatulent Bronx cheer, but the boy was clearly unimpressed. He placed both hands on his chair, lowered his head into the seat, and waved his backside in the air.

"You better quit," his mother said.

When the boy failed to respond, she swatted him on the hip and he winced and scooted out of range. She said, "Didn't I—" but was interrupted by a coughing fit, her chest heaving, her face going red, before she could complete the sentence. The boy took advantage of her distraction and sidled up to Dennis's chair. He was around five, blond, in need of a haircut. He was at once pot-bellied and skinny in the way that only five-year-olds can be.

"You don't look sick," he said, scratching indelicately at the sting left by his mother's slap.

"Well, I'm not," Dennis said. "I'm not sick exactly."

"I'm sick," the boy said.

He coughed once into his fist, as an offer of proof. His display, however, triggered a wave of genuine hacking. He reared back and let fly without a hint of self-consciousness. Dennis cringed and turned his head away.

"Is he bothering you?" the mother said.

"Not too much," Dennis said.

"Pop him if he bothers you," she said. "That's the only thing will make him act right."

She sagged deeper into her chair, let her head tip forward, and shut her eyes. As if for balance or better traction, the boy braced one hand on each of Dennis's knees and coughed directly into his crotch. Dennis spun him around and held him at arm's length until the fit subsided. His mother, Dennis thought, couldn't have been much older than her early twenties. It was clear, even through the pallor of her illness, that she was not an unattractive girl, slim and fair-haired, like her son, with stubborn blue eyes.

"If you're not sick," the boy said, squaring himself, taking Dennis's necktie between two fingers, studying the pattern, "Why you in the hospital?"

"I've been feeling a little woozy," Dennis said.

The boy gave him a cockeyed look.

"What's woozy?" he said.

Dennis took the boy's left hand and guided it to the pecan-sized lump at his hairline.

"You feel that?" he said.

The boy bobbed his head and fingered the knot.

"You ever spin around in circles?" Dennis said. "You know how that makes you feel?"

The boy nodded again, his eyes brightening, as if he hoped that Dennis might suggest a little spinning right there in the waiting room.

"That's woozy," Dennis said.

The boy said, "Do you have a fever?"

"I don't think so," Dennis said.

Gently, with both hands, the boy took hold of Dennis's wrist and steered Dennis's palm to his forehead. His brow was warm, clammy.

He said, "I have a fever of a hundred."

"I can tell," Dennis said.

The boy walked away from Dennis and took a leisurely tour of the waiting room with his hands behind his back. There was something vaguely British and military in his posture. He paused to examine the fishhook in the old man's finger—the old man was reading a *National Geographic* and didn't look up—his lips pursed like he was admiring a masterpiece of art, then gradually, almost incidentally, made his way back to Dennis.

"How'd you get that bump on your head?"

Dennis looked at him a second. The truth was, he'd dropped his razor that morning and hit his head on the sink when he stooped to pick it up, but the truth seemed suddenly silly and small, and he found himself wanting to impress the boy somehow.

"I fell off a horse," he said.

The boy bunched his lips and eyebrows in disbelief.

"I'm a cowboy," Dennis said.

The boy frowned. "You ain't no cowboy," he said. "I never seen no cowboy in no blue suit." He flipped Dennis's lapel.

"Mr. Grayson," the desk clerk said. "Is Mr. Grayson here?"

The old man hobbled over to the Plexiglas window, cradling his wounded hand against his chest.

"You don't believe me?" Dennis said.

The boy shook his head.

"What's your name?"

"Pritchett."

"All right, Pritchett," Dennis said. "I'm going to tell you something and you must promise never to repeat it."

The boy, picking up on the seriousness of Dennis's tone, lowered his voice. "I promise," he said.

"My name is Arturo Sandoval," Dennis said, rolling the Spanish on his tongue. "I am an agent for the Transatlantic Justice Club, and I have dedicated my life to combating evil in all its many forms."

Before Dennis could continue—he hadn't the slightest idea what else to say—Pritchett exploded with coughs, showering Dennis's neck in a mist of spittle. Dennis recoiled, cupped a hand over his mouth, held his breath. When Pritchett had pulled himself together, he wiped his nose with his wrist and gazed reverently at Dennis. He opened his mouth to speak, but Dennis cut him off with a wave of his hand.

"No more questions," Dennis said, warming to the ruse. "I have revealed too much already."

"Tell me," Pritchett whined. "Tell me."

"Name—Arturo Sandoval," Dennis said, eyes front, voice flat and inexpressive. "Rank—major. Serial number—423735919." He gazed over the boy's shoulder. His mother was watching them with one eye closed, and when she noticed Dennis looking, she blinked the other shut as well.

"Mr. Hill?" the desk clerk said. "Where's Mr. Hill?"

"That's me," Dennis said. He stood, listed slightly to one side, righted himself, and covered the twenty feet to the desk in slow careful steps. He lowered himself gingerly into the plastic chair, smiled at the desk clerk. "You're wearing a black beret," he said, wanting for no good reason to endear himself, wanting her to be charmed. "In my family, we have a superstition that it's bad luck to wear a black beret before Thanksgiving." He was surprised at how easily the lie leaped into his mind. It was as if reinventing himself for Pritchett had loosened his imagination. The desk clerk gave him a quick, dismissive glance.

"Just a few questions," she said. "The doctor will be with you in a minute."

Behind him, Dennis could hear Pritchett's mother coughing and wheezing and gasping for air. He made a face at the sound. If the desk clerk heard the noise at all, she gave nothing away.

"Is that contagious?" Dennis said.

The desk clerk shrugged. She was an older woman, closing fast on retirement, her skin papery and fine, the black beret incongruous with her wizened features. Dennis turned to glare over his shoulder at Pritchett's mother and there, just behind and to his right, he found the boy himself. Pritchett was pretending to be engrossed by a mildew stain on the acoustic tile.

"Oh, hello," Dennis said.

"All right, Mr. Hill, let's get this over with," the desk clerk said, launching promptly into her list of inquiries: Was Dennis insured? (Yes.) Did he have previous health problems? (No.) Was he allergic to any medications? (No.) Did he have a history of mental illness? (Not that he was aware of.) When she asked if he was employed full-time (pharmaceutical sales rep), Pritchett said, "Un-un," and Dennis brought a finger to his lips. He gave the boy a look, suggesting magnanimity and enormous disappointment in Pritchett's inability to keep a secret. Then, slowly, he swiveled his head around to face the desk clerk and, in the process, rearranged his features and shook his head to indicate his familiarity with the lovable foolishness of little boys.

"So what is it?" the desk clerk said.

"I sell pharmaceuticals," Dennis said. He looked at Pritchett, rolled his eyes. Pritchett sniggered. "We do antibiotics. In fact"— Dennis bugged his eyes at Pritchett and Pritchett snorted—"this very hospital distributes our products."

Pritchett guffawed, the phlegm caught in his chest, and his laughter turned into coughing.

"What's so funny?" the desk clerk said.

"I have no idea," Dennis said.

He crossed his legs and stared her down. Pritchett's mother shouted, "Pee, you better get over here," and Pritchett took a defiant seat in Dennis's lap.

"All right," the desk clerk said, "what brings you here today?"

"I'm worried that I might have a concussion."

"And why might that be?"

Her voice was simultaneously composed and impatient, a voice used to handling all manner of misguided self-diagnosticians.

"I've been feeling dizzy all morning."

The desk clerk tapped her pen on Dennis's chart.

"Any reason you can think of?"

Pritchett cupped his hand over Dennis's hairline as if to hide the lump. His palm was wrinkled and hot.

"I'd rather not go into that," Dennis said.

The desk clerk sighed and looked at him from the tops of her eyes. "I have to put something on your chart."

"If it makes you feel better," he said, winking at Pritchett, "you may write that I bumped my head." He paused long enough, he thought, to leave a question in the air. "If it makes your job easier, you may write that I dropped my razor and hit my head on the bathroom sink."

Pritchett's mother called again, and this time, he hopped reluctantly down from Dennis's lap and slouched back over to his mother, who welcomed him with two sharp swats on the behind.

Half an hour later, Dennis was stretched on a gurney, waiting for the doctor, one knee up, eyes closed. On his right was a sink and a bank of cabinets. On his left, a flimsy curtain separated him from Pritchett and his mother, and he flinched intermittently at the rasping bass note of their coughs. They sounded, Dennis thought, more like a pair of stevedores than mother and child. A male nurse was trying to get Pritchett's temperature, but, from what Dennis heard, Pritchett was coughing up the thermometer before an accurate measure could be taken.

"Pee, quit," the mother said, worried, irritated. "I'm talking about right now. Let the man take your fever."

"I can't help it," Pritchett said.

"It's all right," the nurse said. "We'll just try again."

"He won't cough this time," the mother said.

This exchange was followed by a brief silence, during which Dennis couldn't help imagining the scene on the other side of the curtain. He saw the mother and the nurse watching Pritchett expectantly. He saw Pritchett holding his breath to keep himself from hacking up the thermometer again. Dennis hoped that Pritchett would foil their efforts for a third time. Eventually, Pritchett coughed and sucked air, and the nurse said, "That's all right. We'll do it rectally instead."

"Rectally," the mother said. "You mean—" She laughed out loud. "You done it now, Pee. You are in for a surprise."

A moment later, the nurse appeared on Dennis's side of the curtain. He was a big man, plump, well over six feet tall, wearing long johns under his scrubs. He smiled curtly, told Dennis he'd be with him in a minute, then searched through the cabinets until he found a rectal thermometer in a cardboard box. Pritchett's mother coughed three times in succession.

"Is she contagious?" Dennis said.

The nurse said, "We're all contagious," then disappeared behind the curtain.

Dennis listened to the nurse and Pritchett's mother struggling with Pritchett's pants; he was happy to note that Pritchett wasn't giving in without a fight. He heard a metallic clatter, and he pictured an IV stand tipping over. Pritchett shouted, "Help me, mister. They trying to put a tempacher in my butt." Dennis knew the boy was calling for him, but he didn't answer. When the noise of struggle faded, he felt unexpectedly ashamed.

"Keep him still," the nurse said, presumably to Pritchett's mother, "while I see about your neighbor." He swung around to Dennis's side of the curtain, washed his hands in the sink, found a blood pressure cuff and a thermometer in one of the cabinets. He took Dennis's temperature—normal. While he was inflating the cuff on Dennis's arm, Dennis asked him, "What did you mean we're all contagious?"

"That's just an expression," the nurse said.

He made a few notes on Dennis's chart. Dennis was curious about his blood pressure, but he figured the nurse would tell him if there was reason to be worried.

"So," the nurse said, "you hit your head on the sink?"

There was absolute silence from Pritchett's side of the curtain.

"I don't know where you got that idea," Dennis said.

"It's right here," the nurse said. "It's right here on your chart."

"Well," Dennis said. "I suggest you have a discussion with the lady at the front desk, because the truth of the matter is that I was mugged at an ATM. I could have been killed."

Pritchett giggled. Then he said, "Ow, Mamma, don't pinch." The nurse cut his eyes to the curtain, then back to Dennis. "Odd," he said, matter of fact, distracted. He made a sheepish face and left Dennis to inspect the situation on Pritchett's side of the curtain.

A long stretch of inactivity followed, during which Dennis passed in and out of sleep. He dozed so easily, so accidentally, he wondered if the hospital wasn't pumping some sort of gas into the room. When he woke for the last time, there lingered, just beyond the boundaries of his recollection, the weird, tawny mist of a dream. He checked his watch; he'd been out for twenty minutes.

He heard Pritchett's mother say, "What's your favorite food, Pee?"

"Ice cream," Pritchett said, his voice drowsy and sad.

"What's your favorite book?"

Pritchett said, *"Goodnight Moon."*

"That's too young for you," his mother said.

"I like it," he said. "It makes me woozy."

"Woozy?" his mother said.

Their voices sifted through the curtain as if from a long way off, and Dennis wondered if the sort of wistfulness he was feeling was a routine by-product of a blow to the head. Goodnight comb and goodnight brush, he thought, Goodnight nobody, Goodnight mush. Those were the only lines he could remember so he improvised. Goodnight fever, Goodnight lump, Goodnight measles, Goodnight mumps. Pritchett's mother coughed. Pritchett followed suit. Dennis heard sticky-sounding footsteps, and a new voice, a woman's voice, said, "I'm Dr. Bob. What seems to be the problem?"

Dennis eavesdropped while Pritchett's mother described their symptoms, her account punctuated here and there by bursts of hacking. Dr. Bob interrupted occasionally to ask a question, and Dennis had the idea that she was examining Pritchett while his mother spoke. At one point, Pritchett said, "Please don't put nothing in my butt," and Dr. Bob promised that she would leave his butt alone if he behaved himself.

"He was sick first," Pritchett's mother said. "I got sick looking after him."

"I didn't mean to make you sick," Pritchett said.

Dr. Bob said, "Do you smoke?"

"I don't smoke," Pritchett said.

Dr. Bob said, "You shouldn't smoke, young man."

In a matter of minutes, it seemed to Dennis, Dr. Bob had diagnosed bronchitis. She appeared on his side of the curtain, found a prescription pad in the drawer beneath the sink, and scribbled for a moment without acknowledging Dennis's presence. Dennis sat up and dangled his feet over the edge of the bed. The room pitched slightly like he was on a boat in gentle seas. Dr. Bob had short spiky brown hair and tortoiseshell glasses hanging by a silver chain around her neck. She lifted the glasses, closed her left eye, and peered at what she had written through the right-hand lens.

Finally, to Dennis, she said, "There seems to be some disagreement about how you hit your head."

"There's no disagreement," Dennis said. "I got mixed up in a liquor store heist. I was pistol-whipped. Wrong place, wrong time, you know. I could have been killed."

Pritchett tittered beyond the curtain.

Dr. Bob aimed the lens at Dennis and raised her eyebrows. She made a clucking sound with her tongue, then whistled, and the nurse poked his head around the curtain. Dr. Bob tore the prescription sheet from her pad.

"Here you go, Biggun," she said. "Give this to the lady next door. Make sure she understands that she shouldn't smoke and that they need to take all ten days' worth of antibiotics, no matter how good they're feeling. Write her a note if she needs to miss a day of work, and I'll sign it when you're done."

The nurse nodded and slipped around the curtain and began repeating Dr. Bob's instructions. "You don't need to tell it all again," Pritchett's mother said. "It's just a curtain. I heard her the first time," but the nurse continued his recitation. Dr. Bob turned her attention back to Dennis.

"You didn't hit you head on the sink?" she said, prodding the knot with her fingertips.

"Nope," Dennis said.

"And you weren't mugged at an ATM?"

"That's crazy," Dennis said.

Dr. Bob sat on the edge of the gurney and crossed her ankles. Her feet hung just short of the floor. Dennis heard the nurse say, "And make—listen to me now—make absolutely, positively sure you take all ten days' worth of antibiotics." Dr. Bob regarded Dennis as if he was a puzzle to be solved.

"That's quite a lump," she said, "however it happened."

She hopped to the floor, her tennis shoes squeaking on the linoleum, and moved in between Dennis's knees. She shined a penlight into his pupils, asked him to follow her index finger with his eyes. He noticed a silver and turquoise ring on her pinkie.

"You don't believe me?" Dennis said.

Instead of answering, Dr. Bob said, "Have you been feeling nauseated?"

"No," Dennis said.

"Tired?" she said. "Sluggish?"

"Not unusually," he said.

Right then, Pritchett's mother let loose a barrage of coughs, and Dennis said, "Is that contagious? Shouldn't I have a mask or something?"

"I can hear you," Pritchett's mother said. "I'm not deaf. What's this gonna cost me anyway?"

The nurse peered around the curtain.

"She wants to know how much," he said.

Dr. Bob said, "Insurance?"

The nurse shook his head.

Dr. Bob sighed and put her hands on her hips and gazed at the ceiling. After a moment, she said, "Tell her the prescription will run about eighty dollars."

"I don't have no eighty dollars," the mother said.

The nurse said, "She can't pay."

Dr. Bob glared at Dennis. She flipped a cabinet open, took out a few plastic packets (Dennis recognized the brand; he had a box of samples in the trunk of his car), then wrote up a new prescription. To the nurse, she said, "All right, Biggun, give her these and tell her they'll get her through the week. But sometime in the next five days, she'll have to come up with the money for the rest of the prescription." When the nurse was gone, Dr. Bob looked at Dennis and started as if she was surprised to find him sitting there.

"What's the date?" she said.

Dennis told her—November 17. She asked for his birthday and he told her that as well—July 22.

"A Cancer," she said. "That explains a lot."

"I don't understand," Dennis said.

"Listen, Mr. Hill, we can do a head CT if that's what you want, but your pupils and your motor skills look good. I don't think that you're concussed."

"You don't?" Dennis said.

"I do not," she said.

"What about the dizziness?"

"Put an extra pillow under your head at night," she said. "Avoid strenuous physical activity for a couple of days. If this so-called dizziness persists, come back and see me."

"You don't believe me?" he said.

"It doesn't make a difference," she said. "You'll be fine. There's not a whole lot we can do for a concussion."

Pritchett poked his head around the curtain just long enough to give Dennis a secret grin, before a hand appeared to snatch his collar and drag him out of sight.

From there, it didn't take long to hustle Dennis past the cashier and back into the world. The sun had vanished while he was inside, leaving misting rain and hazy light in its place. He fished his keys from his pocket and waded out among the endless rows of rain-jeweled cars. He hadn't gone far when he heard Pritchett's mother say, "I'm telling you, Pee, you better get back over here." She was, much to Dennis's surprise, standing beside his Oldsmobile, blowing into her hands. "I'm sick, Pee," she said, her voice tinged with desperation. "It's no good for either of us to be out in the wet."

"He run off?" Dennis said.

She stiffened and, very slowly, turned to meet his eyes.

Her expression suggested that she didn't think there were too many more stupid questions he could have asked.

"I've got him under my coat," she said. "This is a little game we like to play." She swiveled back around to face the parking lot. "Pee," she said. "C'mon now, Pritchett. Please, baby."

"You need any help?" Dennis said.

Pritchett's mother didn't answer.

"He's a nice kid," Dennis said.

The wind pushed at his tie, the part in his hair, the tails of his overcoat. He balled his hands in his pockets and studied Pritchett's mother—her lips chapped, her skin pinking in the wintry air. He walked over to his car and popped the trunk. The trunk was full of boxes of the antibiotic that he sold, along with cases of coffee mugs and pencils and refrigerator magnets and sticky pads and calendars—gifts for the doctors who listened to his pitch. He rounded up a handful of samples and carried them back to Pritchett's mother.

"You win, Pee," she was saying. "I'll leave you if that's what you want." She jangled her car keys on her finger. "Here I go," she said.

Dennis said, "I could get in big trouble for this, but I sell pharmaceuticals for a living, and I've got some antibiotic samples here. They'll save you the cost of a prescription."

She turned, glanced at the packets, her eyes briefly wide and eager. She drew a breath, as if to speak, but was overcome by coughing. When she had collected herself, she licked her lips, flicked a strand of hair from the corner of her mouth.

"We're all right," she said.

Dennis shook his head.

"It's the same stuff the doctor gave you."

"You leave us alone," she said.

Without another word, she walked away, spine straight, hands clasped behind her back, her posture reminiscent of Pritchett's

British military tour around the waiting room. Dennis was left with his arms outstretched, the boxes in his hands, and he had a notion that, to an outside observer, it might have looked like he was asking for something, instead of offering. Pritchett's mother shouted, "All right now, Pee, this is your last chance," and, just then, Dennis spotted Pritchett peeking out from behind the oversized tire of a pickup truck. He almost called out, but he couldn't bring himself to give the boy away.

Mitchell's Girls

Mitchell McRose was vacuuming the living room carpet when he sneezed and threw his back out for the second time that day. The first time, he'd been lugging boxes of research material up from his office in the basement. He'd stooped to set the last box on the kitchen floor and felt a sudden, white-hot pain in the lower part of his spine. He dropped like he'd been shot and lay perfectly still, tiny sparkles dancing before his eyes, sweat beading on his upper lip, until gradually, like a fist unclenching, the pain released him. Since then, he'd mopped the kitchen linoleum, emptied the dishwasher, done two loads of laundry, and put Cassie down for her nap. He had only to run the vacuum—perhaps his greatest accomplishment as a parent was to instill in Cassie the ability to sleep regardless of the clamor in the house—and he could devote what was left of the afternoon to his most recent scholarly project. That was when he sneezed. He attributed the tickling in his nose to a combination of leakage from the worn-out vacuum cleaner bag and extra dust brought up from the basement on his boxes. He knew in an instant that something weird and terrible had happened. The pain was doubled this time—like someone was soldering his ninth and tenth vertebrae together—and his vision faded out and his hands went numb. He sank to his knees, then to his right shoulder, then onto his back, where he'd been sprawled, immobile, for an hour and a half.

He understood, in some more reasonable chamber of his mind, that this predicament was his own fault—after all, he could have left the boxes in the basement and if he hadn't carried them upstairs to begin with, he doubted very much that a simple sneeze would have laid him low and it occurred to him in retrospect that maybe he should have taken it easy for a while after the initial incident and the sneeze itself might have been avoided if he hadn't been exposed to so much dust—but that didn't prevent him from casting about for someone else to blame: his wife, Samantha, for banishing his office to the basement so that Cassie could have the spare room for her own, or his stepdaughter, Tabitha, for being unwilling to share her room with Cassie in the first place, or Cassie herself for being born and outgrowing her crib and requiring a place to sleep at all. He reserved an ample portion of his anger for the chairman of the little history department at the little college in this little nothing town for offering his wife a tenure track position and for Sam's colleagues who never remembered his name—most of them called him Michael when they did bother to speak to him—and for the academic publishing establishment, which had snatched up Sam's dissertation, *Saddle Sores: Syphilis and the Pioneer Women of the Western Plain,* while ignoring his own work on Navajo irrigation technology, all of which was related to the pain in his back only by the fact that, if there was order in the universe and their roles had been reversed, it would have been Mitchell shoving off to teach his classes in the morning, while Sam stayed home to be a mother to the girls.

Three years before he threw his back out, while he was still working on his Ph.D., Mitchell McRose met Samantha Gaylord in a seminar on the French Revolution. She was eleven years his senior and she had about her the allure of tribulation—the pregnancy that cut her graduate studies short the first time around, the vanished husband, the labor of single parenthood. Her story was more pedestrian than he'd supposed, but to someone who had spent his life as a student—it sometimes seemed to Mitchell that he'd progressed directly from the birth canal into the classroom—she was worldly and mysterious and beautiful in the way that Navajo women were beautiful: plain-featured, calloused, unadorned. Because the class met in the evening, Sam brought her daughter along sometimes. They sat together in the back row, Tabitha reading a horror novel, Sam intent on the lecture. When she shot her hand up to ask a question, Tabitha rolled her eyes. Both Sam's enthusiasm and Tabitha's disdain struck Mitchell, under the circumstances, as dear. He was moved in a way he couldn't have explained.

It was Mitchell who insisted that they get married when Sam turned up pregnant despite the fact that she was on the pill— her fertility was as surreal to Mitchell as if she'd been struck by lightning twice—and it was Mitchell who insisted that one of them stay home with the baby. This was before Sam's success, back when they were both shipping out résumés by the dozen and he was morally certain that it was only a matter of time before some university recognized his talent. Even now, he hadn't abandoned his career altogether. He taught a survey every summer to keep his vitae fresh and spent most nights holed up in the basement, Sundays in the research library, cupping his aspirations close to his breast like a small flame in high wind.

Last night, in fact, he'd been down among the cinder block walls and exposed plumbing, plowing through a stack of secondary sources by the light of his bare bulb, when a dollop of condensation beaded on a pipe above his head and plopped onto the pages in his lap. He stared at the runny ink for ten full minutes, years of pent-up frustration and resentment filtering through him like an IV drip. It wasn't that he didn't love his family, not at all, but he saw his situation clearly in that moment, recognized the compromises he had made, the time he'd lost. He vowed then and there to do his work and live his life entirely above ground.

After several agonizing, aborted attempts to stand, Mitchell determined that, if he lay perfectly motionless, the pain in his back subsided to a horrific but bearable ache centered somewhere in the vicinity of his lumbar region. If he so much as blinked, however, if he even breathed too deeply, it radiated to his extremities like an electric current and set his scalp aflame.

And so he gritted his teeth and gazed up at the idle ceiling fan over his head. Its blades were coated with a heavy, gray powder, a combination of various particulates that very much resembled, he thought, crematory ash. Beneath the light globe were the shadows of half a dozen insect carcasses and a lone, still frantic, ladybug. The state of the fan irritated him no end. Mitchell was a scrupulous housekeeper, in spite of his professed loathing of the work, and he couldn't imagine how all that filth had escaped his notice.

A few feet behind and to his right, the vacuum cleaner, which had tipped onto its side when he collapsed, sucked uselessly at the air. For the first hour of his immobility, the noise had been nearly as intolerable as the pain, but eventually, like the whirring of cicadas on a summer night, it faded into the background of his consciousness. Now, Mitchell occupied his thoughts with the plight of the imprisoned ladybug, watched it crawl a centimeter or two up the smooth, inside curve of the globe before losing its footing and sliding down among the husks of its compatriots, where it paused, as if for breath, then took wing, hurling itself like a ricochet against the glass, until, at last, it settled, defeated, in the bowl. Mitchell wondered if the ladybug was aware, on some instinctive level, of the significance of the corpses at its feet.

Later—it might have been a minute or an hour; time had ceased to pass for Mitchell in any measurable way—he heard his daughter over the vacuum and his skin went tingly on his bones. "Daddy," she was shouting, sounding groggy and impatient. He pictured her rattling the guardrail on her bed. "Daddy, I'm awake." Generally, she napped until three o'clock, which meant that his stepdaughter, Tabitha, who was sixteen and too gloomy for extracurricular activities, would be home from school before too long.

The trick, he thought, was to figure a way to keep Cassie in bed and out of mischief until Tabitha arrived.

"Daddy," Cassie said again.

"I hear you," Mitchell said.

"I'm hungry," Cassie said. "I'm wet."

"I'll be there in a minute," Mitchell said.

Much to his surprise, Cassie fell silent, and for an instant he was proud of his little girl, of her obedience, of her patience, but the whine of the vacuum cleaner reasserted itself in the absence of her voice and Mitchell would have sworn that it was louder than before. He combed his brain for a gimmick to keep Cassie busy, a song that they might sing or a story he could tell her, but he couldn't think over the racket or through the pain. Then, quite suddenly it seemed, Cassie was looming over him, naked, one foot on either side of his head. Mitchell had learned, over time, to ignore her private parts and the sight of her genitals eight inches from his face unnerved him. He noticed a stippling of diaper rash before he shut his eyes.

"Where's your diaper?"

He decided not to tell her that he'd hurt himself. He didn't want to make her afraid.

"It was wet," she said. "I took it off."

He could hear the pride in her voice and he had neither the strength to scold her nor the desire to squelch her fledgling attempts at self-sufficiency. He opened his eyes. Cassie looked colossal from this angle, the chubby columns of her legs rising to meet her hips, her belly, her ribs. Her face seemed impossibly far off and he wondered if he wasn't experiencing some kind of tunnel vision as a result of his ruined back.

"You're a big girl," Mitchell said.

Without warning, Cassie sat down hard on his chest and Mitchell, on reflex, lifted his arms to receive her, sending molten rivulets of pain spurting through his bone marrow. He blacked out almost immediately and, when he came to, Cassie was still perched atop his chest, pushing both his eyelids open with her thumbs.

"Daddy?" she said.

She looked concerned, but Mitchell didn't think that she'd been crying. He must have fainted before he'd had a chance to startle her with a scream. He couldn't have been out for long, he thought. Cassie lacked the attention span to stay put more than a minute without a conscious parent or murmuring television to distract her. In fact, he and Sam had recently debated whether or not to have her tested for ADD. Sam was in favor of the tests. Mitchell was not. He believed, with the perfect certainty of the uninformed, that the surge in diagnosed learning disabilities was just one more example of the way society bent over backward to coddle the lazy and inept. Now, Cassie adjusted her grip on his eyelids and said, "Were you asleep?"

"You might say that."

"Are you tired?"

Mitchell sighed. Three feet away, the vacuum cleaner bawled.

"You have no idea," he said. "Let go my eyes, OK."

"Did you take a nap today?"

"Daddy doesn't nap," he said.

"Why not?"

"Please, sweetie, take your thumbs out of Daddy's eyes."

Cassie withdrew her thumbs, settled her left hand on Mitchell's cheek, and pinched his nostrils with her right.

"Why don't you nap?" she said.

Mitchell blinked his eyeballs moist.

In nasal tones, he said, "There's too much to do, I guess."

"How come I don't have too much to do?"

"You're just a little girl," he said.

Cassie released his nose and shook her head. Even that slight motion sent a ripple of pain through him, like warning tremors before an earthquake, and Mitchell's breath caught in his throat.

"I'm a big girl," Cassie said.

"That's right," he said, his voice panicky and constricted. "You're a big girl. That's right. You're right."

"You wouldn't be so grouchy if you took a nap."

"I'm sure that's true," he said.

Mitchell closed his eyes and drew a series of careful, restorative breaths. This was complicated by Cassie's weight on his rib cage. He was afraid that if he strained his diaphragm, he'd pass out again. For a few seconds, he tried to imagine a life in which he whiled away the afternoons beneath cool blankets, nothing whatsoever on his mind, but the relentless hubbub of the vacuum nagged him back into the world.

"Cassie, honey," he said, "can you do Daddy a favor? I need you to—listen now—I need you go over there behind the armoire and yank the vacuum cleaner plug out of the wall." This, he reasoned, was simpler than trying to tell her how to shut it down.

"What's a r-more?"

"It's where the TV lives," he said.

Cassie said, "Oh," and poked his forehead with her index finger, but made no move to stand.

"Please," he said.

"I don't want to," Cassie said.

"I'm begging you," he said. Then, after a moment, already feeling guilty, Mitchell said, "I'll give you a million dollars." He regretted the lie—Mitchell was determined to raise a high-minded child—but the truth was that he'd never felt more desperate in his life.

"You don't have a million dollars," Cassie said.

"How do you know?" Mitchell said.

"You don't have a job."

There was, he knew, no real malice in her remark, but he was devastated nonetheless. He was accustomed to disrespect from Tabitha. They had never managed to settle on a relationship more original than mutual resentment. Even Sam, in the heat of an argument, feeling cornered and hurtful, might have resorted to a cheap shot. But not Cassie, whom he played dolls with by day and read to sleep at night, who turned to him—not her mother—when she was harassed by nightmares. He thought of her as, at least, a temporary ally in a house amok with tampons and cosmetics. In theory, Mitchell understood that Cassie didn't mean to hurt him—she didn't even know she'd hit a sore spot—but he couldn't help feeling betrayed.

"I thought you were a big girl, " Mitchell said.

Cassie was tugging now at the pad of flesh under his chin.

"I am a big girl," she said.

Mitchell said, "I'm not so sure."

Cassie made a face that struck Mitchell as surprisingly adult for a girl her age, her pinched lips and furrowed brow suggesting equal parts disappointment and hostility. Then she rolled to one side and, after the initial wave of pain had passed, Mitchell nearly cried out with relief. In the next instant, however, he imagined Cassie rooting around in the thicket of wires behind the armoire and he realized what he'd done.

"Cassie," he said. "Cassie, wait."

The vacuum cleaner died. The quiet was less a blessing than he'd hoped.

"You all right?" he said.

"I'm a big girl," Cassie said.

"I stand corrected," Mitchell said.

He heard footsteps receding toward the hall and he jerked his eyes around in their sockets, trying to catch a glimpse of Cassie without turning his head. He called her name but she didn't answer. Mitchell guessed that she'd retired to her room to pout. In the light globe, the ladybug was rattling around, stirring the corpses like a hand picking a name out of a hat. Mitchell knew a last gasp when he saw one. A few minutes later, the phone rang and he hoped it might tempt Cassie from her seclusion—she was at an age when she could hardly imagine anything more glamorous than talking on the phone—but the machine picked up on cue. The caller broke off without leaving a message. Eventually, Cassie emerged from her room bearing a fistful of nontoxic markers and Mitchell let her doodle on his face without complaint.

"You look like a freaked-out clown," Tabitha said.

His stepdaughter was more than an hour late getting home from school, but Mitchell was so glad to see her, so thrilled by the prospect of someone to rescue him, that he couldn't muster even a semblance of parental affrontedness. Neither could he let her tardiness pass without remark so, as Tabitha lifted her half-sister from his chest and rested Cassie on her cocked hip, the motion at once timeless and maternal and in perfect contrast to her dyed black hair and the black paste around her eyes, to the rings in her eyebrow, her lip, her nostrils, her tongue, he simply stated the facts. "You're late," he said and hoped that a pardon came through in the tenor of his voice.

"I called," she said. Then, speaking over her shoulder to someone Mitchell couldn't see, she said, "Didn't I call?"

"You called," said a male voice. "She called."

"You didn't answer," Tabitha said to Mitchell, letting Cassie finger the ring in her left nostril.

"As you can see," Mitchell said, "I was indisposed."

"That's not my fault," Tabitha said.

"Aren't you even going to ask me what's the matter?" Mitchell said. His relief at her arrival was fading fast, a more familiar muted fury seeping in to take its place. "Aren't you even going to introduce me to your guest?"

"His name is Dirk," she said.

There followed a sound not unlike the faint clinking of armor as Dirk lumbered into Mitchell's field of vision. He didn't think the boy was much older than Tabitha but it was difficult to tell because his face was painted pale as a geisha and his features were distorted with piercings. He was well over six feet tall, well under a hundred and fifty pounds, and there were delicate lengths of chain through his belt loops and where his bootlaces should have been.

"It's nice to meet you," Mitchell said.

Dirk squinted. "Does that say ass?" he said.

Tabitha laughed out loud. A moment later, like an echo, Cassie laughed, too, imitating her big sister, a recent predilection that plagued Mitchell in his dreams.

Mitchell said, "Excuse me?"

"On your face," Dirk said. "Over your eye."

"Is that supposed to be a joke?"

"No, man," Dirk said.

"He's right, Mitch," Tabitha said. "It looks like ass." She poked Cassie's ribs and Cassie shrieked. "Did you write a dirty word on Mitch's face?" Despite the subject and the circumstances, Mitchell was struck by the playfulness, by the real affection in her tone. It was a manner of speaking she reserved solely for Cassie and it never failed to surprise him.

"Don't call me Mitch," he said, his voice rising in a way that he despised, his temper getting away from him. "And don't encourage your sister. You know good and well Cassie didn't write any dirty word on my face. She's three years old, for heaven's sake. What kind of a person are you? Hasn't it even occurred to you to wonder why I'm laid out here like a corpse? You haven't even bothered to ask if I need help."

Dryly, Tabitha said, "Do you need help?"

"Jesus God, yes." Mitchell couldn't stop himself from shouting. "I've been lying here since one o'clock. The very act of speaking at this volume is as miserable as water torture."

"You can't move at all?" Tabitha said.

"I threw my back out," Mitchell said.

"Hmmm," Tabitha said. She set Cassie down and squatted over Mitchell, her hair falling like a shroud over her face. She fished around in the pocket of her overcoat, produced a wrinkled cigarette, and poked it between her lips.

"Don't you dare," Mitchell said.

Tabitha's eyes glittered behind the curtain of her hair. Dirk stooped to light her cigarette with a Zippo and Tabitha angled the smoke away from Mitchell's face—incongruous courtesies, he thought. To Mitchell, the smoke was redolent of foot odor.

"You promised your mother that you wouldn't smoke in the house," he said.

This, too, had been a bone of contention between Mitchell and his wife. A month before, they had caught Tabitha puffing away in her room and there had been a predictable set-to. Mitchell was in favor of absolutes—no smoking, period—while Sam believed that a parent had to be more flexible than that, had to be willing to expand the parameters of acceptable behavior or else risk losing control entirely. To Mitchell, this reeked of vulnerability and here, he thought, was proof: Tabitha smiling down at him in the living room, wisps of putrid smoke rising from her nose.

To Cassie, Tabitha said, "Do you want to put a cartoon in the VCR?" And Cassie stamped her feet with glee.

To Dirk, she said, "Get us a beer, OK? Guinness. Mitch keeps the good stuff in the crisper." And Dirk trundled off to do her bidding.

To Mitchell she said nothing, and Mitchell shook with rage.

He wanted to launch into a tirade, if only for the sheer release of verbalizing his anger, but he suspected—he could almost hear Sam's voice in his ear—that ranting would be ineffective. This was not to mention the fact that anger had caused his latissimus dorsi muscles to tense, causing in turn a sensation not unlike, he imagined, having his backbone wrung out like a rag. He steeled himself, forced his voice under control.

"I need help," he said.

Tabitha stepped across his body and he couldn't see her anymore.

"Mom'll be home soon," she said.

"Do you hate me that much?" he said. "Can you really stand by and watch me suffer?"

"You threw your back out," she said. "It's not like you had a heart attack."

He heard the creak of the armoire doors, the faint sizzle of the TV, the whirring motor in the VCR. He sensed, more than saw, Cassie getting situated on the rug, propping her face in her hands, absently kicking her legs, and the image made him feel inexpressibly forlorn.

"I'm in pain," he said.

"Mom'll be home soon," Tabitha said again, but Mitchell would have sworn he noted a hint of vacillation in her voice.

"How did we get like this?" he said.

Tabitha didn't answer him this time. He heard the sofa creak as it received her, heard the thunk of her combat boots on the coffee table. He could still smell her cigarette smoke and beneath that, barely, a chemical smell that he thought might be emanating from the product she used to dye her hair.

"Tabitha?" he said.

A question flitted through Mitchell's mind and was on his lips almost before he knew he was going to speak aloud.

"What are you using as an ashtray?"

Tabitha snorted. "It can't hurt that bad," she said. "You're still a prick."

Mitchell knew at once that he had lost her. A moment later, Dirk jangled back into the room, set a pair of bottles on the table—Mitchell could tell from the sound that they weren't using coasters—and dropped onto the couch next to Tabitha. Mitchell felt sick with frustration and pain, but still he kept his composure.

"Dirk," he said, "listen to me a minute. You seem like a decent guy. It's not in your nature to sit by and watch a fellow human being suffer, is it?"

"Well," Dirk said. He paused. Mitchell wondered if he wasn't looking to Tabitha for direction. "The thing is I'm in favor of suffering in many ways. We both are, Tabitha and me. We view self-mutilation as a positive force. That's why the piercings and all, you know. Pain can be very liberating."

At last, Mitchell erupted. "Are you kidding?" he said, each word a knife wound in his back. "Are you out of your fucking mind? You wouldn't know suffering if I shoved it down your throat." He was too irate to care that Cassie was in earshot. "All you've achieved by putting those holes in your face is ugliness. I'll bet you whistle when the wind blows, you little shit." He recognized, even in the midst of his harangue, that he was being cruel, that it was useless, that it was wrong, that they surely wouldn't help him now, but his fury was too enormous to contain. "Don't hand me self-mutilation," he said. "I'll self-mutilate you up and down the goddamn street. I'm in real misery over here."

"That's it," Tabitha said. "C'mon."

Over the music from Cassie's cartoon, Mitchell listened to Dirk plinking down the hall toward Tabitha's room, pictured Tabitha leading him by the ring in his lower lip. Above him, the light fixture was quiet. He watched for what seemed like a long time but nothing stirred. All at once, the anger bled out of him and he felt as if his insides weren't enough to fill his skin.

"Cassie?" he said. "Cassie, you there?"

"I'm a fucking big girl," Cassie said.

Mitchell tried to gauge the time by the quality of light in the room. Since Tabitha's exit it had gone from the watery, gilded blush of late afternoon to a more diffuse and mournful gray. It wasn't dark out yet, but he knew that night was coming soon. He couldn't imagine what was keeping Sam. Cassie's video had played itself out a few minutes before, leaving white noise in its place, and Cassie had left him there alone without bothering to turn the TV off. He had tried to track her progress through the house, but, with the static hissing in his ears, he'd lost the sound of her somewhere around Tabitha's room. He pictured the three of them, Tabitha and Dirk and Cassie, on Tabitha's bed, Tabitha laying out the joys of self-mutilation for his little girl. Worse than that, his bladder had begun to ache.

He shut his eyes, tried to settle himself by breathing slowly through his nose. Last year, Sam had dragged him to her yoga class a couple of times. He'd hated it—all those self-consciously enlightened professors in their pajamas—but he remembered that air flow had been crucial to separating body and mind, to lifting oneself above corporeal needs. The trouble was that breathing through his nose caused a dangerous itching in his sinuses and he began to worry that he might induce another sneeze. The thought sent shivers of pain down his spine and increased the pressure on his bladder and kept him squarely present in the world.

Daylight oozed across the ceiling. The ladybug was dead. Mitchell focused on holding his water. He remembered driving with Sam and Tabitha to the Grand Canyon before Cassie was born, complaining about all the unsynchronized pit stops. They never had to go at the same time and neither of them seemed to have any self-control and, on the last leg, he'd restrained himself for nearly an hour to prove his point. He imagined himself standing on the lip of that vast emptiness, sending an endless stream of piss into the air, and goosebumps prickled on his skin.

The TV static sounded exactly like a waterfall.

His insides burned like he was on the verge of passing kerosene.

He tried, just once, against his better judgment, to stand, but he'd hardly lifted his shoulders off the ground before the pain melted his teeth and peeled the skin off his bones.

Finally, finally, he heard Sam's keys in the front door lock, her heels on the parquet in the foyer.

"Thank God," he said, his voice a plea. Sam kicked her shoes off and padded into the living room. At the sight of her, Mitchell said, "I'm dying here. I really am."

"What happened?" Sam said, crouching beside him, resting one hand on his shoulder. Mitchell winced at her touch. She looked worn-out—her eyes bleary, her makeup patchy, her lips chapped—but still lovely in her way. Her hair was pulled back into a ponytail, her blouse open at the throat, her knees round and tan as biscuits below the hem of her skirt.

"It's my back," he said. "I can't move."

"Where are the girls?" she said.

"In Tabitha's room, I think."

Sam nodded, her eyes crowfooting at the corners. Mitchell could almost see her processing the situation, sizing up the options, weighing various pros and cons. He rushed to fill her in and Sam kept nodding while he spoke, adding this bit of information to her list of considerations, discarding that. Telling the story, Mitchell had to fight the urge to weep.

"I needed you," he said. "You're late."

"I had a conference."

"No one would help me," Mitchell said. He knew exactly how he must have sounded and he detested the self-pity in his voice but he couldn't stop himself. "I was in pain," he said. "I was all alone."

"I'm here," Sam said, "I'll help you now."

She patted his arm, then trotted into the kitchen. He heard her pick up the phone, listened to her discussing his situation with the emergency operator. His bladder boiled. He pictured a distended udder. A minute later, Sam hung up and was standing over him again.

"The guy said not to move you," she told him. "He's guessing pinched nerve, maybe you slipped a disk."

She cut the TV off, the overhead light on, bringing the insect corpses into high relief. Mitchell heard death-throe guitars coming from the stereo in Tabitha's room.

"I'll get the girls," Sam said.

"No," he said. "Wait."

"What is it?"

"I have to pee," he said.

"The paramedics will be here in a minute."

Almost imperceptibly, Mitchell shook his head. After a moment, Sam knelt, brushed his cheek with the backs of her fingers. Her head was cocked to one side, her ponytail hanging over her left shoulder. There were times, Mitchell thought, when the difference in their ages was more apparent, when he remembered just how much longer Sam had been alive. Eleven years was longer than it sounded. In that instant, she looked to him unfathomably wise.

"How long have you been waiting?"

"I don't know," he said. "Forever."

"It's all right," she said.

"I can't," he said. "I won't."

"You'll feel better," Sam said.

She leaned in close and pursed her lips and blew cool air across his brow. Like magic, the muscles in his groin relaxed. Mitchell felt the damp heat of his urine spreading against his leg. The sensation seemed peculiar, remote, like he had at last transcended his earthly self, and he realized, then, that he was crying. They felt connected, his swampy crotch and leaking eyes, as if Mitchell was brimming over.

Sam thumbed his tears away.

"There," she said. "OK?"

Mitchell didn't answer. He was still beyond himself somehow, dissolved and hovering—history was just history; the past was just the past—and he saw the light fixture looming through his tears like an enormous, hospitable star, felt himself rising toward it, believed that if he uttered even a single word he would be sucked backward and down again into a world in which everything was born to die.

"I'll get a towel," Sam said.

Ellen's Book

1. Every day, my wife and her mother drive down from the house in Ashland Place and eat lunch in Bienville Square. And, every day, I steal away from work and spy on them from the window of the drugstore across the street. My wife has been staying with her parents since she left me. Sunlight filters through the big oaks, drawing liquid shadows on her face and bare shoulders. Nearby, a quartet of old men is playing cards on a stone table. Ellen shakes her head, gives her mother a careful smile. I have no idea what they are saying. I only know that they are not talking about me. Mrs. Allbright, in her yellow sundress and walking shoes and old-lady bracelets, believes that bad things can be held at bay by leaving them unspoken. I watch Ellen finish eating and stuff a Tupperware bowl into her purse, watch her stand and smooth her shorts over her hips. I can see from here that the wrought-iron bench has left an intricate tattoo on the backs of her legs.

Ellen is barely five feet tall, but she moves like she's much taller, nothing but slink and skin and bones. Look there. The wind has snagged a paper napkin, and Ellen is dancing after it over the bricks.

I have decided to write a book about my wife.

2. Kosgrove Construction hires temps for on-site secretarial needs, and I've been called in to handle the filing and answer the phones. They're building a new middle school out by the airport. The land has been cleared, foundations poured, but this afternoon, the work has been delayed by bad weather. Through the window in the

trailer, I can see the level, silvery expanses of concrete where the classrooms will one day stand, but so far it looks more like something destroyed than something in progress, torn-up ground, pools of rain water reddened with clay. Everything's quiet. Most of the construction crew has moved to a site where there is indoor work to do. I swipe a hard hat from the supply shed, tour the naked rebar and the rubbish heaps. The rain beats down on my shoulders. On the slab of what will be the cafeteria, I find the words *Henry Was Here* pressed into the concrete. Henry is the name Ellen would have chosen for our child.

3. My wife is a long-suffering insomniac. When she was a little girl, she lived in fear of missing something important while she slept, something cryptic and adult, the unedited solution to some antique mystery. After we married, she would glide out of bed when she couldn't sleep and rewrite my stories on the word processor in the spare room. Ellen found my fiction bland and deliberately remote. The men in my stories, she said, leaned too far toward emotional distance. She filled my bleak, ironic little numbers with romance. Brief glances became revelations of love. Missed opportunities, for better or for worse, were nearly always acted on, and her characters could, at least, fade into the final paragraph without regret.

4. I call late enough that everyone should be asleep, but Ellen's father is manning the phones. He sounds groggy, maybe a little tight, and I can hear strains of classical music in the background. Wade Allbright is of the opinion music begins and ends with Beethoven.

"Keith?" he says. Then, "Jesus," when he understands that it's only his daughter's estranged husband on the line, and his family is safe, and this not one of those awful after-midnight wake-up calls.

"I didn't mean to bother you," I say. "I was hoping Ellen would answer."

Wade chuckles softly, like he has been in my shoes before, like I'm just in the doghouse and all this will soon be a memory. That isn't true, I know, but I find his voice immensely reassuring. He had, I imagine, dozed off in his big leather club chair with a glass of scotch in one hand and the stereo remote in the other.

"She said you might be calling. The fact is, pal, she doesn't care to speak to you right this minute."

Ellen's father is one of those old Alabama smoothies who can talk friendly no matter what sort of bad news he is delivering.

"She'll call Wednesday," he says. "Just like last week."

My wife has not cut off communications entirely. She has agreed to one phone call a week, always, for some reason, on Wednesday, and always at the hour of her convenience. She believes that, in this way, she can achieve an honest separation, without ruling out the possibility of reconciliation. I'm not pleased with the arrangement, but I take what I can get.

"How's she doing, Wade?" I say. "Is everything all right over there?"

"It's been rough on her," he says. "She doesn't sleep much. You know this isn't what she wanted."

"I know," I say.

We are quiet for a moment, married men contemplating women in the waning hours of the night. Into our silence, string music swells. Wade is fiddling with his remote.

"You ever hear Beethoven's Quartet in F Major?" he says.

"I wouldn't recognize it," I say.

"Deep," he says. "Goddamn." Ice clicks against his teeth. His chair creaks lavishly. When he says, "Nobody listens to Beethoven anymore," there is real sadness in his voice.

I will treat Wade Allbright kindly in the book.

"I'm sorry for all this," I say, but it's no use because he's covering the phone with his hand. I can make out a muffled voice in the room with him, maybe my wife's, maybe her mother's.

"I have to hang up," he says. "I'm under orders."

"I understand," I say.

I'm lying in bed while we finish up. Old Dog is beside me, his head on Ellen's pillow. We rescued Old Dog from the pound. He's a medley of breeds, weighs about as much as Ellen. Sometimes I wake in the middle of the night with Old Dog breathing on my mustache. I walk him outside, and both of us whiz into the boxwoods. The mustache is new. In the book, I'll have copious facial hair as a way of revealing something important about my character.

5. In part, Wade Allbright blames himself for getting his daughter mixed up in a failing marriage. He owns and operates a string of car dealerships out by the interstate, and his receptionist quit, without warning, to start a hemp farm in the foothills of North Alabama. Wade phoned for a temp to fill in while he interviewed for a full-time replacement.

That's where I come into the story.

Ellen was working for her father on the management end. She was just a few years out of college. Wade's employees treated her with the fondness and deference generally reserved for young children. I suspect her size played a part in their good will. She moved through the garage aswim among the elbows of large men. They spoke to her in soft voices. They tousled her hair with oily hands, and Ellen never seemed to mind. She remembered their names. She knew their histories. I'll need to come up with a more evocative phrase for the final draft, but, to my eyes, she was charmed.

She even took the time to introduce herself to temps.

"I only do this to pay the bills," I said, thumbing the telephone headpiece. "I'm a writer. I write fiction."

I nodded seriously, my armpits going clammy. We scanned the showroom as if the perfect subject for a novel were unfolding before our eyes.

"I always liked to write," she said. "I signed up for a class over at adult ed last year, but everybody was always so depressed."

We did all the usual getting to know each other—marathon phone calls, kissing in public, you name it. Eventually, we wound up in my bed. My brain was a haze of endorphins and adrenaline and whatever else your glands are churning out when you're in the middle of falling in love.

"My sister was an accident," Ellen said. She pushed the sheet down around her midriff. "Beth is sixteen years younger than me so I got to watch my parents raise a child. It was like home movies. There's a story in there somewhere."

"You'd have to add some tension," I said, feeling the pulse in her wrist with my fingers. "The first time around the couple was happy and young. Things have soured over the years. They were planning a divorce until the second child. Maybe something like that."

"No tension," Ellen said. "This is a happy story." She pinched the hairs below my belly button, then swung out of bed and minced through the room in the dark looking for her clothes.

6. Mornings, I wake up early and stare at the computer, trying to imagine a beginning for Ellen's book. Dreary light slants in through the blinds, my shadow is pudgy at my back. The whole time I have the feeling that I'm being watched, but it's not Old Dog. He's snoozing in the kitchen. The hair on the back of my neck goes squirrelly. Goosebumps, etc. I take a break to check beneath our bed and paw through the closets. I peel back the mildewed shower curtain. I rattle knobs to make sure I locked the doors.

*   *   *

7. My wife is watching TV through the display window at Barney Electronics. Her mother has ducked inside to use the restroom. They are on their way home from lunch in Bienville Square. Misting rain, but they stuck it out, polished off a pair of sandwiches beneath a red umbrella. Have I established the season? Late spring, pleasant despite the weather. I am hiding behind a bakery truck, gathering my nerve. If the truck pulls out before her mother returns, I will speak to her. If not, a meeting isn't in the cards. Ellen in a navy blue raincoat, her toenails painted silver beneath the hem.

In the book, Ellen will be cagey and sad, always just beyond the reach of my understanding.

Then the truck pulls away, leaving me crouched on the damp pavement, my hair slicked over my skull. I wobble toward her on the sidewalk, behind and to her left, watch my reflection come even with hers in the plate glass, which is a nice detail. Ellen is intent on the TV and hasn't spotted me yet. At that moment, past our shapes on the window, I see her mother moving toward the door and I dodge behind a mailbox on the corner. I hear the bell announcing her exit, hear her mother say, "Were you talking to someone? I thought I saw a man with an undergrown mustache."

Right away, I'm in a flopsweat. If Mrs. Allbright was close enough to notice my mustache, surely she was close enough to recognize her son-in-law. But Ellen says, "No, I wasn't talking to anybody," and Mrs. Allbright says, "I would have sworn," and I think maybe she wants me out of her daughter's life so bad that her eyes refused to see me there.

8. I tell people that I'm still temping because it leaves me several days at a stretch for my real work. The truth is my real work amounts to a handful of short stories, only one of which has been published. It was picked up by a feminist literary journal called *Virginia's Room,* and that was an accident, more or less. I posted one of Ellen's re-

writes by mistake. I should have suspected something when I read the letter, which said, "The prose is uneven, but I started crying on the first page of 'Satellite' and didn't stop for two days. How is it possible for one man to know so much about women?"

9. The Tuesday Night Prayer Group meets in a bar called Roget's Downtown. The name, a play on the actual Bible study meetings that convene all over Mobile, was Lamont Turner's idea. Lamont is a short story writer who takes great pride in his agnosticism. There are four writers in the group—Lamont, Richard Frost, Brenda Mayo, and myself—and we have published exactly three stories between us, though Brenda is nearly finished with her autobiography and, because she was raised by an abusive father then went on to marry a drunken bully, we have high hopes that she will find an agent. Tonight, we are hashing out the idea of a book about my wife.

"Would you publish?" Lamont says.

"That's beside the point," I say. "She'll see it before then anyway. The real question is, will it win her back?"

"How long would it be?" Richard says.

Richard is the youngest in the group, maybe twenty-four or twenty-five, a graduate student at the state university here in town. He has a sinister goatee and his work is strictly hypertext.

"Does that matter?" I say.

"It could," Brenda says. "Your wife might be tempted to draw a correlation between the number of pages and the scope of your emotion."

"Is everyone so hung up on length?" Lamont says. He finishes his drink and signals the waitress. "Why wouldn't a short story, perfectly drawn, serve your purpose just as well?"

I shrug, not wanting to get into this particular line of discourse. Lamont has an inferiority complex regarding the short story. We put the discussion on hold while the waitress takes orders for another round. When she's gone, Richard says, "You're talking about fiction, right, a sort of parallel universe? Maybe you should use footnotes, you know. To draw the analogy between your real life and your book life."

"I don't want footnotes," I say. "I want my wife."

Brenda brushes her lips with a finger. She says, "Wait a minute, now, Richard has a point. Why not just do the whole thing as a piece of creative nonfiction?"

"That wasn't my point," Richard says. "What I was talking about was layering the text."

"Layering the text?" Lamont says, his voice gluey with loathing. He is looking at me when he says, "Does that even mean anything? Isn't anybody interested in craftsmanship anymore?"

We sit without speaking for a few seconds, all of us nodding solemnly, a moment of silence for the death of craftsmanship. The waitress arrives with new drinks, beer for Brenda and myself, bourbon for Lamont, red wine for Richard Frost, and waits for one of us to indicate that the time is right for an interruption. She is young, almost pretty, her legs descending from her shorts into white socks and running shoes.

"I couldn't help but overhear," she says. "I think it sounds great. The book about your wife. That's the most romantic thing I ever heard." She smiles at us, and we smile back. The moment keeps stringing itself out. "My name's Mandy," she says.

I say, "Well, hey, Mandy, thanks for the kind words."

"I really do think it's a good idea," she says. She gathers the empties, retreats to the bar. We peer grimly into our drinks. Finally, Richard excuses himself to go ask Mandy for her number.

10. Ellen and I had been together for seven weeks when she missed a period. We bought a drugstore test, and she was pregnant. I asked her to marry me because it was the right thing to do, and, to my surprise, she smiled and said she would, without giving it

much thought. It was as if no one had explained to her that a bad thing can happen in this world.

"But do you love me?" I said.

We were sitting cross-legged on the grassy strip of median in the parking lot of my old apartment complex. Ellen was barefoot, the sky crazy with stars.

"Sometimes," she said.

"Like when?" I said, still dumbstruck.

She laughed and punched my chest, then realized I was serious and composed her face into a thoughtful frown. "Like last week," she said. "You were at the kitchen sink rinsing a mug."

11. Ellen calls while I'm in the shower, and I barefoot down the hall in a hurry, toweling my head on the way.

"Hey," she says. "It's Wednesday."

Her voice sounds long distance. Old Dog picks through the mess on the bedroom floor and settles at my feet. He groans, like negotiating discarded clothes is the most difficult thing he's done in a long time. Old Dog's arthritis stiffens a little more each year, and rain makes him ache.

"The dog wants me to ask when you're coming back," I say.

A long quiet follows, and I imagine all the subjects we're avoiding backing up in the phone line like a gridlock. The clock beside the bed reveals that I'm running late for work.

Ellen says, "This is hard, Keith."

The simplest statement in the world and I don't know how to respond. I scratch my new mustache, rub my chin whiskers against the receiver. In the book, I'll have to smooth the edges of this scene, fill my head with thoughts too numerous, too painful for utterance, but for now, I lie back on the bed, hoping Ellen will mistake my silence for cogitation.

"Is this connection funny?" I say. "I can hardly hear you."

Ellen does an exacerbated sigh, so familiar I can see her face, the amused lips, the crowfooted corners of her eyes. "Mom?" she says. "Hang up the phone, Mom."

I hear a click, quiet as a whisper, and the line clears. "She's just worried," I say.

Ellen doesn't answer, but I can picture her nodding a reply. Sometimes, my wife forgets she's on the phone and goes ahead with all sorts of nonverbal communication. She's in her old room, I think, her view pretty houses and big magnolias. She can hear traffic sounds drifting over from Dauphin Street. Maybe she is hiding in her closet like when she was a girl and she wanted to make a call in secret.

"I've been writing," I say, which sounds awful and self-important the moment the words are out of my mouth, but Ellen wants to know what it is I'm working on.

"A story?" she says.

"I don't know yet," I say. "I'm just taking notes."

Old Dog creaks upright and swipes halfheartedly at his neck. He is winded by the effort. His muzzle is all winter, his eyes rheumy and sentimental. Somebody should write a story about Old Dog.

"How about a sneak preview?" Ellen says.

Beyond the window, rain falls gently on the neighbor's hydrangeas. I close my eyes. I promise Ellen she'll be the first to read it when I'm done.

12. Ellen's version of "Satellite" is about a young woman married to a man incapable of tenderness. It's simple, poignant in a heavy-handed way. The wife is pregnant, worried and unhappy, but she loves him and she wants to make a go of wedlock. She sends signals and makes loaded remarks. What she needs from him is a grand gesture. The husband, a top astrophysicist, finally gets the picture. Everybody's happy in the end. The principal

metaphor features a moon in lonely orbit around a heedless planet.

The wife has a bit part in the original. My version is about mankind and its place in the mysterious universe.

13. My Taurus dies on the way to work, and I have to hoof the last couple of miles to the Kosgrove site. The grass is knee-high beside the road, threaded with Queen Anne's lace and black-eyed Susans. Nobody notices that I'm late. I call a tow from the trailer and wait for it in the misting rain. The driver turns out to be a black guy, closing in on sixty. His name, according to his license, is Muhammad Ali. "Like the boxer," I say and Muhammad Ali goes, "Heh, heh." As we're leaving the site, headed back to my car, I see the word *Henry* spray-painted yellow on a Porta-John.

14. Ellen and I told her parents about the baby on Good Friday. Mrs. Allbright wept for her daughter's innocence and for the baby, conceived in a union not sanctified by God. Wade took me aside and offered me a permanent position at Allbright Motors. I refused—graciously—on principle, and I think he respected me for that. Almost a year has passed. Those, I think now, were the happiest hours of my life.

15. Because the Taurus is in the shop and I haven't yet figured out the city bus schedule, I missed Ellen in Bienville Square today. I settle for a view of her bathroom window. The Allbrights' house is only a couple of miles from mine, but even that's too much for Old Dog. He is napping, exhausted, at my feet. I watch Ellen scrub her face, her skin luminous and pale, her hair held back with a bandanna. She smears lotion on her cheeks and gives her toothbrush a workout. I watch her bare her teeth at the mirror, check-

ing her handiwork, the way she has done every night that I have known her, but tonight, my heart is a ricochet in my chest. There is something intimate about looking in on her like this, something thrilling, as if I am on the verge of discovering my wife in a way I overlooked before.

Ellen kills the bathroom light, and I nudge Old Dog awake with my foot. He moans and looks at me like that's too much to ask. "All right," I say. I gather him in my arms and carry him to a magnolia with a view of Ellen's room. Her sister, Beth, follows Ellen in, wearing matching pajamas and slippers, and sits beside her on the bed. Ellen lets Beth brush her hair. Beth gabs excitedly, but Ellen's answers seem cursory from my vantage. Her mind is elsewhere. After a few minutes, her mother appears in a nightgown. When she speaks, her daughters laugh, and for an instant, Ellen looks happy.

Wade's women, the Allbright girls.

I notice, then, that Old Dog has realized why we're here. He is peering intently through the leaves at the scene beyond the window.

"Sorry, pal," I say. "I'm not welcome."

Old Dog couldn't be more disappointed. He whines, beats his tail against my legs. Mrs. Allbright guides Beth out of Ellen's room, and Ellen heads over to the window. The dog looks at me with pained eyes. I don't think Ellen can see us, but I crab into the bush just in case. Ellen lets her brow drop against the glass. Her breath makes and erases ghostly ovals on the pane.

16. Ellen was three months pregnant on our wedding day. We said our vows on the elegant stairway in her parents' house. Despite the circumstances, Wade spared no expense. We could hear the orchestra tuning up during the ceremony, harried caterers putting the finishing touches on the menu. Late in the afternoon, I snuck upstairs to Beth's room and watched the reception on

Wade's pristine lawn. Below me, dapper guests strolled from one tent to the next. The grass looked impossibly, unnaturally green, and the whole day had a vaguely underwater feel. Ellen moved out from beneath a yellow awning and I watched her lift her dress with both hands to keep the hem off the grass, watched her rise up on her toes to scan the crowd. She's looking for me, I thought. I thought, there is my wife.

17. Thursday night, Lamont calls an emergency meeting of The Prayer Group, which is to say he's drunk and he wants company. Roget's Downtown is mostly quiet, and Lamont and I are alone at the bar. Brenda couldn't come. Her Battered Wives Team meets on Thursday to discuss their various tragedies. Richard Frost, however, has arrived and is making out with Mandy at the waitress station. He has somehow convinced her he's a genius.

"Admit it," Lamont says, "you think because I only write short stories my stuff is less important." He is verging on bitter and morose. He is breathing open-mouthed, his lips moist, his eyes haggard. He grabs my wrist on the bar top. "Look at Carver, you bastard. Look at Raymond-fucking-Carver."

"You're a good writer," I say.

His features go soft all of a sudden. His eyes water up. He turns away before he starts to cry.

"Do you believe in ghosts?" I say.

Lamont doesn't hear me. He can't take his eyes off Richard and Mandy, Richard's hands up Mandy's shirt, Mandy's pretty mouth disappearing into Richard's beard.

"I'm considering a subplot for the book," I say. "I don't know how it'll fit. It's about a dead baby haunting his father. He feels like he's being watched all the time and he sees his baby's name in weird places. Stuff like that. I don't know. Maybe it won't work."

But I'm talking to myself.

"He's got the whole package," Lamont says, his voice weary with sadness, his gaze still fixed on the action down the bar. "The shaved head. The glasses. He's got the goatee. Women always think geniuses have goatees."

18. For several hours after I finished reading Ellen's version of "Satellite," I seriously considered proposing a joint literary venture. Together, I thought, we were capable of publishable work. I wanted her to know that half a talent was the worst thing in the world. That sort of ordinary can't help but break your heart.

19. Friday, I wake to the sound of Wade Allbright's voice, rise through layer upon layer of sleep to hear him barking orders on my lawn. It is as if I have slipped into a dream of yardwork.

"Right here, Pedro," he says. "The grass needs cutting, the hedge needs a haircut, and this azalea bed needs new mulch."

"Angel."

"What's that?" Wade says.

"My name is Angel. The old head groundskeeper, he retired last year, his name is Pedro."

"Mucho apologioso," Wade says. "Your name is An-hell. I want all this ragweed vamoosed by nine o'clock, An-hell. No telling how long the rain'll hold off for us today."

I open the window and hang my head outside, and there is Wade, in a short-sleeved shirt and striped tie, his hands on his hips, marshaling a trio of Hispanic yardmen.

"What time is it?" I say.

"Pushing seven," he shouts. "I brought my crew over from the dealership. Thought we'd give this yard a spruce." He storms over to the window and peers inside. The room is a masterpiece of disarray. Dirty clothes, dirty dishes, reams of wadded paper around the bed. "The house could use a once-over, too, looks like. Where's the car?"

"Alternator's busted," I say.

He gives me a hurt look. "You should've called me. When's it coming back?"

"Monday," I say.

"Monday my ass," he says. "How're you getting around?"

I say, "Bus." And Wade says, "Jesus on a Popsicle stick, Keith. What if Ellen was to come by here this morning? Where's your head, boy?" He jabs his index finger at me. "Listen up," he says. "I'll send Lavinia round for the house, and somebody from the dealership will handle the car. Now, get dressed. I'm driving you to work."

I pull myself together in a hurry, wet my hair in the sink, dump some food in a bowl for Old Dog, who is dozing in the kitchen. I'm ready for Wade in nine minutes flat. Ellen's father is a big man, his frame softened by easy living. I like him all over again, because he doesn't try to drum up conversation on the ride. Neither does he mention my new mustache, for which I am grateful, because it has arrived at something like a larval stage of growth. We cruise without speaking, past the strip malls and the hospital, Beethoven's Fifth murmuring from the tape deck.

"Take him," Wade says, tipping his head toward the dash. "There's a fella had some serious adversity between himself and beautiful music."

He is referring, I suspect, to Ludwig van Beethoven, but I decide to keep my mouth shut until I'm sure.

"Ellen is a mess sometimes," Wade says. "I know that. And nobody could have helped what happened."

He shakes his head, raps his wedding band on the wheel. Sweat is beading on his upper lip. He's having a tough time. I tell him what I meant for him to hear the other night.

"I'm sorry for all this, Wade."

He exhales a yard of pent-up breath. "Lord in Heaven," he says. "This is my daughter we're talking about."

20. Ellen delivered a stillborn male child near the end of the sixth month. I was temping for a locksmith when she went into labor. Because of a mix-up at headquarters, I didn't get the news for several hours. I barreled into the birthing room just in time to witness Dr. Hershey emerging from between Ellen's knees, and I keeled over on the spot and woke in the hospital with Ellen in bed beside me. She was small enough that she fit on the strip of mattress between my body and the edge. The room was dark, except for a green light from a monitor by the window.

"Are you awake?" she said. "I thought I heard you wake up."

"I'm awake," I said.

"Do you remember fainting? Dr. Hershey said you looked like a vaudeville routine." Her voice sounded so matter of fact I wondered if I hadn't cooked up the scene in the delivery room from scratch. She propped herself on a elbow, ran her warm instep along my calf.

"I didn't mean to faint," I said.

"It doesn't matter," she said, and I knew, then, that what I remembered—the limp, slick, membranous creature—had nothing to do with my imagination. I could just make out Ellen's face, her features bunched and overserious like a little girl. This will be a big scene in the book. The decayed flower smell and the sterile half-light. The cross-hatched shadows. The dreadful, animate heat of our bodies side by side.

21. The good weather unleashes bedlam at work—everybody on the double to make up for lost time. I've got a phone at either ear most of the morning, one hand in the file cabinet, the other hack-

ing out shipping manifests on the computer. While I'm polishing off the payroll, I come across the name Henry M. Hotchner, and it occurs to me to do a little sleuthing over lunch. There are three Henrys on the crew, it turns out—Hotchner, Shiflett, and Breedlove—and one by one I track them down. The day is all evaporation, the sun delirious with rediscovered strength. Each Henry looks at me like I'm crazy when I ask if he's the one who's been writing his name, and each in turn denies it. The last guy, Hank Shiflett, is a crane operator. He's got porkchop sideburns and a pompadour beneath his hard hat.

22. I wrote this sentence when I was eighteen: *After dinner, he knelt beside her chair without a word and rubbed her feet.* It was a story about old people. It's not much, I know, but it made me want to write another. I'll make myself a happy-go-lucky ad man in the book. I'll have new suits and pressed shirts and polished shoes.

23. The doorbell rings just as I'm selecting a Hungry-Man from the freezer, and I pad down the hall, carrying my dinner like a schoolbook. The peephole offers a blurred, compressed view of the yard, newly groomed, and the flagstone path that leads to my front steps. Prank, I think, neighborhood kids. I play along, crack the door, prepared to look angry and confused, and right then Ellen's hand flashes through the opening, and she catches me by the hair of my mustache.

"It *was* you," she says.

She spins me around by the lip and backs me against the wall, paralyzing me with pinprick pain.

"I mibbed you," I say. "I lub you, Ebben."

"Hell," she says.

Finally, Old Dog lumbers to my rescue. He wedges feebly in between us, slaps his tail against Ellen's thighs, shoulders his way through her legs. If he was a younger man, he would bear her to the ground with the weight of his affection. Ellen has to release my mustache to keep her balance. I press the frozen Hungry-Man against my lip.

I say, "What tipped you off?"

"Daddy mentioned your new look," she says. "Mamma saw a man with a mustache. I put two and two together."

"I'm sorry," I say.

Ellen keeps her eyes on Old Dog, runs her fingers through his fur until he collapses, spent, on the hardwood and offers her his belly. His eyes droop shut, his tail winds down. I crouch beside them and get to work on his rib cage. Ellen thumbs a wayward bra strap out of sight.

"You still writing?" she says.

"Yeah," I say. "It's a love story."

Ellen flicks her eyes across my face and back to Old Dog. "Does it have a happy ending?"

"I won't know until I get there."

Ellen pushes to her feet then, her business concluded, and we stand in the hallway looking at each other for a long moment. Instead of working on the book, I should have been dreaming up a phrase or two for right now, here in the present tense. The air is full of birdsongs. My neighbors are bantering pleasantly across back fences. Mothers are calling their children home. Everyone knows their lines but me.

24. Most nights, Old Dog eats his dinner in front of the television. When he's finished, I take him for a walk. We drift around the block, past quiet porches and American flags and bird feeders in the trees, pausing now and then to peer up at the stupid stars. A neighbor's terrier greets us, without fail, as we make the last corner, and Old Dog runs her off with a rumble in his throat.

"You've still got it," I tell him.

That wretch, Old Dog, wags his tail.

25. Wade Allbright brings the Taurus around himself on Saturday. He must do his best work in the early morning because the sun is just pushing over the horizon when he barrels into the driveway, the horn, mysteriously, blaring Beethoven's "Ode To Joy." Old Dog groans and makes a face, scandalized by the hour of the visit.

Wade beats me to the door, lets himself in with his key. We meet in the front hallway, and he brushes by me, headed for the kitchen.

"Did I wake you?" he says.

"I was up," I lie, despite the boxer shorts and the bleary eyes and the pillow-addled hair. He is still my father-in-law, after all, and I want to make a good impression. Wade is sporting tennis duds, a white sleeveless sweater over a blue shirt and white shorts, his grizzled old man's thighs still broad and muscular. I ease myself into a seat at the breakfast table, watch him pushing canned goods around on the shelf above the range. It seems he has plans to make of pot of coffee.

"I had my wiring guy put the horn in last night," he says. "That's Beethoven."

"Thanks," I say.

"I'm only gonna say one thing. I am aware Ellen dropped by yesterday. We're not even gonna get into that. I didn't mean to blow your cover, but Ellen is under the impression that my sympathies lie with you. I want to be sure you know how wrong she is."

"All right," I say.

"I like you, Keith," he says, "but she's my girl. If she asked me to come over here twice a day and beat you silly with a Wiffle ball bat, I'd start keeping one in the Lincoln, know what I mean?"

Ellen's father understands the simple algebra of manliness. I wonder if Wade has ever found himself so reduced by a pretty girl. In fiction, a tidy parallel might ordinarily come to light at this point. Wade would admit that he had stalked Mrs. Allbright for months before she finally gave in to his affections. But on this day, with the pristine light against the window, with the insects chattering in the grass, all we have between us is the terrifying memory of bachelorhood.

"How did you and Mrs. Allbright meet?" I say.

He pauses, a coffee filter pinched daintily between two fingers.

"We were kids," he says. "It's not a very good story. I saw Annie at a public swimming pool."

Old Dog lurches into the kitchen, then, and flops onto the tile at my feet. Wade shakes his head.

"How old *is* that dog?" he says.

"We don't know for sure," I say. "He was old when we got him. The vet puts him somewhere around fifteen."

Wade returns his attention to making coffee. He fills the pot with water, measures out the grounds. There is an order to the way he works, deliberate, personal. He is, I suspect, in charge of handling the morning coffee at the Allbright residence. When his preparations are finished, he sits across from me and rubs his face with both hands. He says, "Did you know Beethoven was deaf as a tree stump when he wrote his Ninth?" I nod, and he says, "That always made Ellen cry when she was little."

26. Marriage, as I had known it, ended on a Monday. Ellen was standing over me at the breakfast table in the kitchen. I was eating cereal and slipping Old Dog bacon slices that Ellen had undercooked. Neighborhood sounds. The way Ellen smelled in the morning, like newspapers, like a memory of soap. Newsprint

on her fingers. Her fingers around a coffee cup. A coffee cup pressed against her sternum.

"This is sad," Ellen said.

I followed her gaze to the window, hoping she was referring to something in the backyard, the coiled garden hose or the mildewed picnic table, which did look somehow sad in their way. I avoided the obvious question. I knew what she meant. We had been biding time. This was three months since the hospital. I shoved off to work every morning and at night, Ellen stayed up late so we wouldn't have to be alone together in the dark. In between, I could be found hiding in the spare room, tapping, like this, at the keyboard so Ellen would have something to work on when insomnia kept her from her dreams.

"Everything's fine," I said. "Nobody's happy all the time."

I set my spoon in the bowl. Ellen collected my dishes, scraped uneaten bacon into the trash, spilled leftover milk into the sink. She ran the faucet and rinsed her hands. I'll need to handle this moment carefully in the book. Had I only recognized the importance of the morning, had I only known that an hour later she would be packing, an hour after that she would be gone, I would have penciled myself in a better man.

27. Due to paranoia and grave loneliness, I have no luck at the computer. I punch up a sorry sentence, sweep it away with the delete key, then hack the very same sentence out again. I write and erase, write and erase, etc. All the while, I can feel eyes on the back of my neck. I whirl in my chair, but the room is empty except for me and my nasty writer's block. I creep sock-footed to the door and leap into the hall ready for a confrontation, but there is only Old Dog napping on the rug. The eyes follow me everywhere and remain just over my shoulder no matter how fast or which direction I turn.

At noon, I pack it in and hike to the Dew Drop for an oyster loaf and fries. There, I find *Henry loves* scratched into the surface of my table like the writer was interrupted in mid-defacement. My fingertips go electric. I ask the waitress how long the words have been there and she frowns and says, "Maybe an hour, maybe twenty years, who knows?"

The sky is a confusion of yellow light. The eyes escort me home, past a black woman and a white man watering an overheated radiator, past an oak cracking the sidewalk with its roots. When I shut the door behind me, Old Dog peeks around the corner, sees it's only me and flops down, already snoring, in the hall. I climb into bed and draw the covers to my neck and dial the Allbrights' number on the phone. Ellen's mother answers on the first ring. In a spontaneous British accent, I ask if I might have a word with Ellen, but Mrs. Allbright says, "You aren't fooling anybody, Keith. You know Ellen doesn't want to hear your voice."

"Please, Mrs. Allbright, put her on for just a minute. I'm having a peculiar day."

"That doesn't surprise me," she says.

Yesterday, per Wade's instruction, Lavinia, the housekeeper, whipped my bedroom into shape. My sheets are clean and cool. The dirty clothes have been laundered and put away. I wriggle down beneath the blankets, but, even still, I have the prickly sense of being watched.

"I owe you an apology," I say. "That was me at the electronics store. The man with the mustache. I should have spoken."

"I don't know what you mean," she says.

Already, she has erased the sight of me from her mind.

"It doesn't matter. Listen, would you ask Ellen something for me? Please, Mrs. Allbright, it's more important than it sounds."

"What is it?" she says, her voice tired.

Annie Allbright is not a cruel or unfeeling woman. In the book, I will have to put myself in her shoes. From her point of view, I must look like nothing less than the agent of her daughter's ruin.

"I want to know if she believes in ghosts," I say.

"I will ask her no such thing."

"I love her," I say.

"That may be true," she says, "but it doesn't make a difference."

Mrs. Allbright breaks the connection, leaving me hiding in my marriage bed, miles and miles of silence on the line.

28. When I told Ellen about "Satellite" and *Virginia's Room,* she was weeding in the backyard. Her face was showing the faintest hint of chloasma, plum blotches on her cheeks like she was blushing all the time. Mask of pregnancy, her mother called it. Ellen was four months gone. She told me not to bother informing *Virginia's Room* of our collaboration. I could have the credit, she said, she'd only been messing around. She wiped her forehead with the back of her hand, smiled a harmless smile. For some reason, all this made me angry—the smile, the modesty, the flawless generosity. I wanted her to understand that what the two of us had done, even if we never managed to do it again, was a rare and wonderful thing.

29. Saturday evening, the Allbrights hit the Carmike for a new release. From behind a huge, freestanding cardboard movie advertisement, I watch them load up on popcorn and Milk Duds and Diet Pepsi. Wade pulls out a wad of bills and complains good-naturedly about the expense. His daughters bump shoulders, pretend to be embarrassed, his wife wags her eyebrows. They have each heard his take on concession prices a hundred times. From my hiding place, I love them all. They weave across the crowded lobby. Wade, popcorn in one hand, soft drink in the other, props

the theater door open with his hip, and the women file past, Mrs. Allbright and Ellen and Beth, and Wade falls in behind them in perfect formation.

I know from experience that Ellen's bladder will drive her from her seat in a few minutes. If I'm lucky, she'll be by herself. The lobby empties gradually. The ticket taker abandons his window until the next seating. For a while, it's just me and the girls at the concession stand. Then, maybe a half hour into the movie, Ellen emerges alone and trots across the carpet toward the restroom, and I follow, wearing my most innocent face, the very face of a man who might wander into the ladies' room by mistake, but no one pays me any mind. Inside, I locate her sandals and take the adjacent stall.

"Please don't be mad," I say.

"Nope," Ellen says. "This is not happening."

From two stalls over comes a delicate, "Eeeck," then the sound of a handbag being gathered up and the click of heels on tile. The door wheezes on its hydraulic arm.

Ellen says, "If I were you, I'd be in a hurry to leave."

"Keep me company until security gets here," I say.

"I'll do what I came for," she says. "That's all." Her urine trickles into the bowl. "I thought being in the bathroom together gave you the creeps."

"It doesn't give me the creeps," I say. "I just don't like to think of you having worldly needs."

"That's a problem," she says.

She spins the toilet paper roll and flushes, and I watch her jeans rising up her legs. Her feet vanish one at a time, then her face appears above the stall, her fingers curled over the divider. She grimaces at the sight of me, hops down from the toilet and heads for the row of sinks. I listen while she washes her hands. From the lobby comes the murmur of impending commotion.

"Do you believe in ghosts?" I say.

"What?"

She shuts off the water. I can picture her at the bank of mirrors, dusting her eyebrow into place with her little finger. In narrative terms, I think, this is a pivotal moment. The bland, watery light. The pleasant echo of her voice. But before I can repeat my question, the door bursts open. This is not theater security. Somebody has called in the pros. I get to my feet, just as the stall is kicked in toward me, catching my forehead on the backswing. A female cop, built like a phone booth, fills my woozy frame of vision. She goes for my hair, and I flinch, which, apparently, makes her angry because her next move is a knee to the face, followed promptly by a headlock, and before I can get a word in edgewise, I'm pinned to the floor with my hands cuffed somewhere up above my shoulder blades and her boot on the back of my neck.

30. Ellen left while I was still at work. I found Old Dog languishing in the kitchen. Taped to the refrigerator was a note: "I'll call Wednesday. You break my heart." That was easily the most terrifying piece of prose I'd ever read.

31. Prison is about what I would have expected, the holding cell all painted yellow bars and cinder block walls, iron benches on three sides, occupied by an assortment of second-tier criminals, most of whom are sleeping or swapping lies with the hookers in the women's cell across the way. The only thing that's missing is a toilet in the middle of the room, but in this jail, prisoners are escorted one at a time to a unisex number down the hall. This is good material, I think. It's my first time in the big house—as they say in crime novels—and I want to take it all in, the wet rag smell, the way the guards and the regulars bullshit like old friends.

In the last two hours, I have stood in line for fingerprinting, had my possessions inventoried and confiscated, and been issued a pair of loose cotton pants, a too-small white T-shirt, and plastic flip-flops for my feet. Now, I'm lurking in the corner, studying the band of pale skin where my wedding ring has resided for the last nine months.

Beside me on the bench is a black man, wiry and bald, vaguely familiar. He has been eying me since I sat down.

"Drugs?" he says.

"No thanks," I say.

He says, "Naw, man, like this: I'm aggravated assault on a not-paying-his-bill-busted-up-car-motherfucker, heh, heh. White guy look like you usually possession."

"I was arrested in a ladies' room," I say.

"Pervert," he says. "I gotcha."

I decide not to argue. His hand, knuckles big as class rings, is spread flat on the bench. At that moment, I notice *HENRY WAS FRAMED* scratched ragged in the paint beside his thumb. The hair on my neck bristles. My heart cranks up. I point and say, "Did you write that?"

"You been here longer than me tonight," he says.

That's when I recognize him—Muhammad Ali, my tow truck driver from the other day—and I'm instantly at ease. My blood slows down. My legs go weak with strange relief. The world is thick with coincidence, I think. These *Henry*s have been here all along. I'm primed to notice them is all.

From down the hall, somebody shouts, "O'Dell, Keith, you made bail," which is surprising since I've yet to use my phone call.

I drift toward the bars, then down the long corridor and up the stairs to find Wade Allbright seated in the lobby. He sees me coming, shakes a handful of leftover Milk Duds into his palm.

"You all right?" he says.

"I feel great," I say.

He double-takes, decides to ignore me. I sign some papers at the desk. We walk outside together. Wade opens the passenger door, and like a cop, he eases me in by the back of the neck.

"Ellen's at the house," he says. "She wanted to check on the dog."

I beam at him despite myself. I say, "Thanks for bailing me out, Wade. I can hardly believe how well everything's coming together."

Wade shuts the door and walks around the front of the car, tossing his keys from hand to hand. He climbs in beside me and shakes his head.

"You're a weird kid," he says.

32. Our contributor's copies of *Virginia's Room* arrived in a manila envelope last week. I haven't told Ellen yet. There is a barechested woman in a ski mask on the cover. It looks symbolic but I don't get it. Maybe Ellen will be able to tell me what it means.

33. Here's what passes for an ending these days:

The first thing I notice when Wade drops me at the curb is that the front door has been left open and all the lights are on. Right off the bat, I think Ellen has swiped the dog and vanished from my life forever. I watch Wade's taillights receding down the street. I head up the front steps. There is no Old Dog to greet me at the door. I think, this book is not turning out how I had hoped. I think, this was supposed to be the scene in which I win her back for good. Then, in a narrative turn too perfect to believe, I hear what sounds like mumbling in the bedroom. I'm around the corner in a hurry, and, in the flicker of light from the whispering TV, I behold Old Dog and Ellen side by side in bed. She must have dozed off waiting for me. Old Dog slaps his tail gently on the mattress. Clearly, he wants to let her sleep.

"Shhh," I tell him.

I retrace my steps without making a sound. For a long time, I sit at the kitchen table doing exactly nothing. I'm with Old

Dog. It's enough to have Ellen in the house for now. She might be gone again tomorrow. After a while, I dial Lamont Turner's number on the phone. He's always up late, always working. He does his best writing in the middle of the night. When he answers, I say, "How do you regard the epiphany in fiction?"

"It's bullshit," he says.

"That's what I thought," I say.

Lamont hangs up, and I make the rounds of the house. When the doors have been secured and all the lights are off, I sneak into the room, stretch out beside my dog and my wife. Half-asleep, Ellen murmurs, "I want to shave your mustache in the morning."

Blackout

Porter and Franny Caldwell were watching a human interest segment on the ten o'clock news when, less than a mile away, a dead branch sheared away from a hundred-year-old oak and fell across a string of power lines, drenching the neighborhood in darkness. They sat for a minute without speaking, the world perfectly quiet, the night holding its breath. Then the dog started barking in the backyard and Porter cleared his throat. He said, "I've forgotten—" He cleared his throat again. His voice felt oddly out of practice. "I've forgotten where we keep the flashlight."

"It's in my nightstand," Franny said. "I'll get some candles."

They left the room in opposite directions, Franny padding toward the kitchen, Porter feeling his way down the hall to the bedroom. Halfway, he stepped on something sharp and metallic and had to grit his teeth to keep from crying out. When the initial shock of pain had passed, he picked it up and held it close to his face—Franny's earring, shaped like an aspen leaf. He put the earring in his pocket and shuffled his feet the remaining distance to her side of the bed. He found the flashlight, carried it over to the mirror and shone the beam under his chin, turning himself into a ghoul, cheeks sallow, eye sockets dark, then followed the beam back down the hall. The living room was aglow with candles when he returned, light and shadows lapping at the walls. Franny was at the bay window, hands cupped around her eyes. A few days before, she'd had her hair cut short—she had come to believe that, at thirty-one, she was too old for ponytails—and Porter wasn't used to the sight of her neck.

Franny said, "Does the phone work in a blackout?"

"I don't see why not."

He walked over to the window and stood beside his wife. The glass held the reflection of the room, a half-dozen tiny flames and the two of them, Porter in his suit pants and his undershirt, Franny in a white sleeveless blouse and linen shorts. Out back, the dog, Tonto, was still barking, plaintive and insistent.

"Maybe I'll call Rhonda in a minute," Franny said.

Porter made a face. Rhonda and Wyatt Miller had recently purchased the brick bungalow next door. Rhonda had a tan and pendulous breasts and yellow hair. Her idea of funny was to ridicule her husband. Franny found her charming. Porter worried about the influence she might be having on his wife.

"In a minute," he said.

He slipped his arm around Franny's waist and leaned in to kiss her neck but Franny shied away and braced a hand against his chest.

"Quit," she said.

"It's romantic," he said.

"I'm worried about Mrs. Hildebran," she said. "I couldn't see any lights on in her house." She gestured at the window. Mrs. Hildebran, long ago widowed, lived across the street.

"The power's out," he said.

"I'm talking about candles," Franny said. "I'm talking about a flashlight."

"Mrs. Hildebran's asleep," he said.

Franny said, "I'm calling Rhonda."

"It's this new haircut," Porter said. "You're like a different woman."

"But I'm not ovulating," Franny said.

Porter sighed and drew her toward him but she ducked out of his grasp and picked up a candle and carried it toward the kitchen. He heard her pull a chair back from the breakfast table, heard her lift the phone down from the cradle mounted on the wall. After a moment, she said, "Rhonda? Me," and Porter headed for the bathroom. He'd stashed a pack of cigarettes in a Band-Aid box. He wasn't supposed to be smoking. Nicotine, according to Franny's doctor, affected his sperm in a way that Porter didn't understand and might have been the reason they were having trouble getting pregnant. He'd cut down to a couple of cigarettes a day, but he couldn't quite bring himself to quit. Now, he tapped a cigarette from the pack, stuffed the pack into the box, put the box behind a stack of towels in the linen closet. He took the book of matches from the toilet lid, tiptoed out into the backyard. Tonto stopped barking to trot over and lick his hands. Porter hid behind the potting shed to light his cigarette. It wasn't that he didn't want a family. It pleased him, in fact, to imagine the house awash in baby smells, to see himself dark-eyed and haggard from a long night with a restless infant, but this vision of his life seemed far removed from the methodology and disappointment of recent months. Franny had presented him with dozens of pamphlets and he'd read them all, but he was unable to shake the notion that a child ought to be born of something more spontaneous and grand.

Franny couldn't stop herself from whispering. "You can see him?" she hissed and Rhonda said, "I'm wearing Wyatt's night vision goggles."

Rhonda Miller was six years Franny's senior, relocated from Houston to Mobile against her will because her husband had accepted a transfer to the local office of a national paper mill concern.

Franny said, "What's he doing?"

"It looks like he's smoking," Rhonda said.

Franny was surprised by Porter's smoking, too surprised for the moment even to be angry. Mostly, she didn't want Rhonda to know that her husband was keeping secrets.

"Where's Wyatt?" Franny said.

"He's in the garage looking for these goggles. He was preparing to search the house for evidence of my affair when the power went out."

Franny twirled the phone cord around her finger.

"Will he find anything?" she said.

"Not without his goggles."

"You're awful," Franny said. "What did you do?"

"I didn't do anything. I didn't have to. I just stopped answering the phone when he calls home from work. Then I give him flimsy excuses when he wants to know where I was. He's jealous as hell. We'll be back in Texas by September." Franny heard Rhonda muffle the phone, heard her shout, "Try the attic then," her voice thick, muted, faraway. To Franny, she said, "That asshole. He wants me to help him look."

Franny giggled. The Millers had only been in the neighborhood for a month but already she had grown fond of Rhonda, of her daring and irreverence. Franny sometimes wished she could be so unrestrained.

"Why's he have night vision goggles in the first place?"

"You know Wyatt," Rhonda said. "He's an idiot. He reads sniper books. He gets these military surplus catalogs. We used to have all this Vietnam junk, but now it's Persian Gulf." She paused. "I better run. He'll tear the house down in a minute."

Franny hung up and carried the phone over to the window above the kitchen sink, the cord trailing out behind her like a tail. Across the street, Mrs. Hildebran's house was bathed in shadow. Porter was probably right, she thought, Mrs. Hildebran was in bed when the blackout settled in. Right now, she was dreaming her way to morning. Even so, Franny couldn't help feeling worried. Mrs. Hildebran was eighty-something, her husband dead, her only daughter way up in Chicago. She had lived in this neighborhood for fifty years, had survived its decline and its eventual renewal, young couples buying up the old houses for next to nothing and breathing life back into them, replacing rotten siding, refinishing the floors. Franny weighed the thought of waking Mrs. Hildebran against the possibility that she was alone and afraid in the enveloping night and dialed the number. The phone rang sixteen times before she disconnected.

Porter dipped the cigarette into the standing water in the bird-bath, flicked the butt into the Millers' yard, and trotted up the back steps. Tonto started barking the instant he closed the door. He listened for a second. When Tonto paused to catch his breath, he heard another dog answering. He couldn't tell how far away it was, but it might have been miles. Porter thought it was the saddest sound he'd ever heard. He padded down the hall and found Franny leaning against the kitchen sink, holding the phone against her chest. He was startled again by her haircut, so neat, so boy-ish, exposing the pale curve of her ears, making her neck look slender and long and vulnerable. She reminded him of hieroglyphs he'd seen of ancient Egyptian queens.

"I want you to do me a favor," she said. "I want you to go over and look in on Mrs. Hildebran."

Porter rubbed his eyes.

"Franny," he said.

"I'm serious," she said. "I'm worried."

"I told you," he said. "Mrs. Hildebran's asleep. I'll go over there and wake her up and the only person who'll feel better about anything is you."

"I called," Franny said. "She didn't answer."

Porter took a bottle of scotch down from the cabinet, located a clean glass in the dishwasher, filled it halfway. "She's old, Franny. I'm sure she just didn't hear the phone."

"Porter," she said, her voice rising and thinning in such a way that he thought she might be close to tears, "Mrs. Hildebran's a nice woman. She brought us a pound cake when we moved in and she made us a pecan pie when you helped her mulch her flower bed that time. I don't ask for much. I don't even complain that you're out in the backyard smoking when you told me that you'd quit and you know smoking is awful for your fertility. It seems like the least you could do is—"

"All right," he said, "I'll go," and he took her in his arms because she really had started to cry. She was small and brittle against his chest. He felt a surge of guilt—he hadn't actually tried that hard to quit—then he wondered how she'd known he was out there with a cigarette and he guessed that she'd been spying and his guilt was diluted by a sudden flare of anger. He considered raising the issue but thought better of it and stroked the new stubble on her neck instead. Franny sniffed, wiped her eyes on his shoulder.

"I'm sorry," she said. "I'm just worried."

"It's all right," he said.

"I'm not mad about the smoking," she said.

"You'd have every right to be," he said.

"I read in a magazine that most people fail at least three times before they manage to quit for real."

Porter sipped his drink over her shoulder.

"I should have told you," he said.

Franny stepped back and gave him a teary-eyed, conciliatory smile. She traced her finger down his breastbone.

"You'll check on Mrs. Hildebran?" she said.

The phone rang the instant Porter shut the door behind him and Franny hustled back to the kitchen to pick it up, stubbing her pinky toe on the way. She sucked air over her teeth and was hopping on one foot when she answered, her vision blurred by a second wave of tears.

"What's wrong?" Rhonda said. "What's happened?"

Franny leaned against the wall and massaged the bones in her foot until the pain began to ebb. "I stubbed my stupid toe," she said. "What about you?"

"Wyatt's coming over there," Rhonda said. "He couldn't find anything in our house to yell at me about so he's headed your way to complain about the dog."

"What's the matter with the dog?" Franny said.

"Nothing's the matter," Rhonda said. "He's barking, that's all. Wyatt's just not happy unless he's pissed."

Porter had left his drink on the counter and Franny limped over and brought it to her lips, her eyes welling up again as the scotch ran down her throat. Darkness pooled in the corners of the room. Franny clucked her tongue. Now that she'd been reminded of Tonto, she could hear him baying over and over like he'd cornered something wild.

Halfway across the street, Porter heard a man's voice calling his name. He brought the flashlight around, the beam wobbling across magnolia leaves and reflecting on windows, and he saw a shirtless figure in striped pajama pants, wearing what looked like some kind of android mask, flat-eyed and metallic with black straps running over his skull. He aimed the light at the man like it might slow him down.

"Who's that?" he said.

The man said, "Can't you do something about that dog?"

"Wyatt?" Porter said. "That you?"

"That dog is driving me crazy," Wyatt said.

He stopped at the border of his lawn, hands on his hips, his chest and arms rippling with musculature, a pelt of hair dark against his pale skin. Porter lowered the flashlight.

"What's that on your head?" he said.

"Night vision goggles," Wyatt said. "Flashlights are for chumps."

Porter looked at the puddle of light around his feet.

"Hunh," he said.

They were quiet for a moment. Porter switched the flashlight off. The night was cloudless, the moon a luminescent bulb.

Tonto loosed a volley of barks then hushed, insect noises rushing in to fill the silence.

"Hear that?" Wyatt said.

He stepped into the street, his upper body tilted forward as if bracing himself against a stiff wind.

"I hear him," Porter said.

"What're you gonna do about it?"

Porter sighed. He didn't care for Wyatt Miller—he was loud and rude and burdened with muscle mass—but they'd been thrown together on occasion by Franny's friendship with his wife. Generally, they managed to be civil, but Porter suspected that Wyatt returned his dislike, and the truth was, the man made him more afraid than he wanted to admit. "How's this?" he said. "I'm on my way to check on Mrs. Hildebran, but I'll bring the dog inside when I get back."

Franny drained the first scotch while listening to Rhonda describe her husband's obsession with his physique, poured another couple of fingers and knocked that back as well, a shudder creeping over her skin, while Rhonda inventoried in minute, acerbic detail the way he varied his routine to isolate particular muscle groups.

"It's because he's so short," Rhonda said.

"How tall is he?"

Franny wiped her mouth, splashed more scotch into her glass and returned to her chair. She hadn't had a drink in seven months, no wine, no beer, no anything, on the chance that she might come up positive on a pregnancy test. Now, with her vision softening at the edges, all the planning and self-imposed restrictions, all the vitamins and ovulation charts seemed as ridiculous as Wyatt Miller measuring his body fat.

"He swears he's five six," Rhonda said. "But I'm five six and I've got an inch on Wyatt flat-footed."

"Do you like the way he looks?"

"He looks great," Rhonda said. "The way he looks is not the issue."

Franny swung her legs up into the seat of a second chair, crossed her ankles, let herself slide forward into a slouch.

"What about Porter?" Rhonda said.

"He looks all right," Franny said. "He's a little soft around the middle."

Rhonda said, "At least he can pass a mirror without tearing his shirt off and making kissy faces at his reflection."

Franny laughed and Rhonda did too. When they'd settled down again, Rhonda asked Franny which actor, living or dead, she thought would play her husband in the movie of his life.

Much to Porter's irritation, Wyatt Miller followed him across the road and up the steps to Mrs. Hildebran's front porch. He jerked his head side to side like the night vision goggles were illuminating ghosts that Porter couldn't see. Porter looked in through the windows, saw only darkness, and reluctantly mashed the button for the doorbell.

"It's electric," Wyatt said.

"What?"

"It's electric," Wyatt said in an exasperated voice. "Power's out." He twirled his finger in the air beside his head.

"Oh," Porter said. "Right."

Wyatt jerked the screen open and began pounding on the door and Porter reached out and caught his arm.

"That's an old woman in there," he said.

Wyatt scowled. "You want to stand here whispering until she gets up to fix her morning coffee?"

Because of the goggles, Wyatt's mouth was his only readable feature—his lips suggested barely suppressed rage—and it made Porter uncomfortable not to be able to see his eyes.

"Just wait a minute," he said. "Maybe she heard you."

Wyatt grunted and let the screen slap shut. Porter sat on the porch steps. Hanging ferns dangled webby fronds above his head. Porter could sense Wyatt looking at him, but refused to meet his gaze. Wyatt linked his fingers, cracked his knuckles.

"Let me ask you something," he said. "You're over at First Mobile, right? Trust department?"

"That's right," Porter said.

"What kind of hours do you keep?"

"Regular hours," Porter said.

"I figure you're pretty much nine to five, but it'd be easy enough to take a long lunch now and then, sneak out the office a little early?"

"I suppose," Porter said. "Why?"

"No reason," Wyatt said.

He crossed the porch, leaned against the rail, his weight on his hands, the muscles in his arms taut and well-defined, and he gazed with augmented vision into the night.

Franny's left ear was feeling hot and bruised so she switched the phone over to the right, but it felt clumsy on that side so she returned it to its original position. "And you really don't think there's another way to get Wyatt to take you back to Texas?" she said, turning a careful pirouette in the kitchen, the phone cord vining around her calves.

"Did he ask me if I wanted to move to Alabama? I don't think so. Did he ask me how I felt about giving up my life? He did not."

"It just seems a little mean," Franny said.

"It's not mean," Rhonda said. "Feeling jealous will remind him that he loves me, that's all. It's not as if I'm really cheating on him. A little jealousy will remind him that I have options and he should take that into consideration the next time he wants to turn everything upside-down."

When she was completely bound up by the cord, Franny stopped turning and began taking mincing steps the other way to free herself. She almost asked Rhonda why she stayed with Wyatt in the first place—she didn't know what a person could see to love in that man—but she stopped herself in time and rephrased the question.

"What's so great about Texas anyway?" she said.

"You've never been to Texas?" Rhonda said. "Oh, honey, everything good in this world comes from Texas."

Franny tipped her glass back, drizzled the last few drops into her mouth.

"Like what?" she said.

"Well, there's barbecue and oil and country music. There's Tom Landry and Morton Salt."

"Morton Salt comes from Texas?" Franny said.

"You bet," Rhonda said. "They're up in Grand Saline."

Franny listed toward the pantry, found a cardboard tube of Morton Salt, took it down, and read the label. What Rhonda said was true. She wedged the phone between her cheek and shoulder and sat on the linoleum, glass in one hand, salt in the other, her back propped against the refrigerator door.

"How come you and Wyatt don't have kids?" she said.

When Wyatt couldn't stand waiting any longer, he crept around the back of Mrs. Hildebran's house to check the windows there and Porter watched him go, hunched and stealthy, moving on the balls of his feet along a row of mahonia, his skin luminous in the moonlight. Minutes passed. Darkness swirled and eddied in the recesses of the porch like it was taking advantage of the blackout to reclaim the night for good. Behind him, Porter heard the

thunk of a dead bolt, the rattle of a chain. He stood, expecting to
see Mrs. Hildebran, and was so startled by the sight of Wyatt Miller
at the door, one hand on the knob, goggle lenses glinting, that he
missed a step and stumbled and landed on his backside in the
yard. He bounced to his feet and brushed himself off, his face
burning with equal parts anger and humiliation.

"That was pretty funny," Wyatt said.

"Never mind how funny it was," Porter said. "Where's
Mrs. Hildebran? Is Mrs. Hildebran all right?"

"I haven't seen her," Wyatt said. "There was a key under
the mat."

Porter gaped. "And you took that as an invitation? Is there
something the matter with your head?"

"You're the one wanted to check on her," Wyatt said.

He pivoted on his heel and disappeared into the house.
Porter didn't know what else to do but follow. He trotted up the
steps, tiptoed across the threshold, nearly bumped into Wyatt from
behind. Wyatt brought a finger to his lips. They crept forward in
single file.

"How well can you see in those things?" Porter whispered.

Wyatt stopped and raised his fist like a soldier walking
point. Before Porter had a chance to say another word, he sprang
around the corner into the hall, landed hard enough to shake the
window panes, and Porter heard what he would have sworn was
the crumple of a body hitting ground.

Franny decided that if Porter could have a drink on a Tuesday
night, she could have as many as she wanted. After all, she didn't
have to get up early for work in the morning and she'd been
denying herself all this time while Porter sneaked cigarettes in the
backyard, and the blackout itself, as remarkable in its novelty as
an unanticipated holiday, seemed to call for celebration. But no
more scotch, she thought. All that scotch was beginning to make

her queasy. The talk of salt made her think of tequila, but tequila left her wrecked so she resigned herself to rum and Coke.

"Any fool can have a baby," Rhonda said.

"Don't you want to be a mother?" Franny said, tugging open the refrigerator, momentarily taken aback by the darkness inside. Then she remembered that the power was still out, found a liter bottle of Coke, and shut the door in a hurry so the cold wouldn't escape.

"Why should I?" Rhonda said. "No money, no sleep, no time for yourself. You hear all these people talking about what a joy it is, how they can't describe the feeling. It's like you're being recruited by a cult. And how they look at you—like you're so pitiful."

Franny was disappointed. She understood this point of view, of course—she had, until not so long ago, felt much the same way—but tonight, she had hoped to enlist Rhonda as a sympathetic ear.

"You don't ever think you're missing something?"

"Listen," Rhonda said. "There are enough babies in the world without me. I mean, do I strike you as particularly maternal? And Wyatt? Lord. Can you imagine that jackass with a child?"

Mrs. Hildebran was sprawled on her belly in the beam of Porter's flashlight, her nightgown bunched around her thighs. Her legs were gaunt and mottled with stubble and liver spots and veins and Porter wanted to cover them, but he couldn't bring himself to get too close. Wyatt crouched at her side, pinching her wrist between two fingers.

"She fainted," Porter said. "Jesus Christ."

After a moment, Wyatt said, "I don't think she fainted."

Porter ran through the likely chain of events: Mrs. Hildebran had been on her way to answer the door, when Wyatt jumped her and she swooned from fright. That, Porter could understand—with his night vision goggles and his squat, hairy, overmuscled body, Wyatt must have looked like some kind of goblin, the living embodiment of old-lady nightmares.

"Of course she fainted," Porter said.

Wyatt dropped her wrist and shook his head.

"I don't feel a pulse," he said.

"That can't be right," Porter said. "Feel again."

"You feel," Wyatt said.

"I don't want to feel her," Porter said. He looked at the back of Wyatt's head, black straps cutting furrows into his crew cut. "Would you take those ridiculous goddamn goggles off. I think now would be a good time to start acting like a normal human being."

"Don't boss me," Wyatt said.

Porter waved the flashlight.

"Are you kidding me? Is that some kind of joke?"

"This isn't my fault," Wyatt said.

"I didn't break into her house," Porter said. "I wasn't the one jumping around like a goddamn ninja lunatic."

"I suggest you zip it," Wyatt said.

For a moment, neither of them spoke. Even from this distance, Porter could hear Tonto making a racket across the street. The sound put him in mind of Morse code, a series of clipped barks, a high-pitched yelp, a long, watery howl, primitive and complicated at the same time. He felt the weight of Wyatt's pronouncement settling over him—no pulse. Wyatt leaned against the wall and rubbed up and down to scratch his back.

"I'm gonna hurt that mutt," he said.

"That's great," Porter said. "That's real constructive."

Wyatt balled his hands.

"I want to ask you something," he said. "I want to know where you were last Thursday at three o'clock."

"What are you talking about?" Porter said.

"Just answer the question," Wyatt said.

"How am I supposed to answer that?" Porter said. "You expect me to remember where I was at some random time in the middle of last week when right this minute there's a poor old dead woman on the floor?"

"That's what I thought," Wyatt said.

In one quick motion, he drew his arm back and swung and his fist caught Porter squarely on the nose, startling the flashlight from his grasp. It clattered to the floor, winked out. Porter tottered backward, tasting blood in his throat, his vision swimming. He dropped onto his hands and knees and Wyatt punched him in the back, folding him up, shoving the air out of his lungs. He loomed over Porter for a moment, then stepped across his body and left him in the dark.

Franny was perched atop the counter, her heels thumping the cabinet doors. "I want to have a baby," she said, and after a few seconds, in a bored voice, Rhonda said, "I don't see what for."

"I can't help it," Franny said. "It's what I want."

"If you say one word about your biological clock, I'm coming over there to pour a bucket of water on your head."

Franny hopped down from the counter, her drink lapping over the edge of her glass and onto the back of her hand. She sucked at the pad of skin between her thumb and index finger and tried to recall the moment she had made up her mind to become a mother, the strange magnetic pull of her desire, but it seemed hazy and faraway just then, an almost forgotten fragment of a day-old dream.

"It's hard to explain," she said.

"What about Porter? What's he want?"

Franny said, "I thought I knew."

"Uh-oh," Rhonda said.

"You know you saw him smoking before? Dr. McCourt told me that smoking is rotten for his fertility—it makes his sperm sluggish or something—and Porter promised me he'd quit."

Rhonda guffawed into the phone.

"What's so funny?" Franny said.

"His sluggish sperm," Rhonda said. "I'm picturing a bunch of tired old men limping up your cervix."

"That's not funny," Franny said. She wondered what was keeping her husband, wondered why Wyatt Miller hadn't arrived to complain about the dog. She walked over to the window and shaded her eyes to see past her reflection. The sky was comic book black and the houses across the street, Mrs. Hildebran's among them, were silhouetted against it, windows glowing weakly here and there like jack-o'-lantern eyes.

Porter lay on the floor for what felt like a long time, his nose clotted with blood, his back throbbing, tiny red stars dancing before his eyes. When the pain had subsided some, he rolled onto his knees, groped for the flashlight. His knuckles brushed the dry skin of Mrs. Hildebran's arm and he shuddered. He could see a vague outline of her body, her nightgown picking up what little moonlight found its way into the hall.

He turned away from her, inched his trembling hands over the rug. His fingers closed over the flashlight handle. When he pressed the button, nothing happened. His blood jumped. His skin was oily with sweat. He held his breath and shook the tube, batteries rattling, and it came winking and stuttering to life, the beam swinging over Mrs. Hildebran—he noticed that her dentures had been jarred crooked by the fall. He switched the light off again, pushed to his feet, staggered quickly down the hall. He dialed 911 on an old rotary phone in the living room. After a moment, detached and toneless, an operator said, "Please state the nature of your emergency."

Porter didn't know how to answer. He might have made sense of his presence in the house—his wife sent him, they found a key, not so hard to understand. He might even have explained the body—she was an old woman, after all, prone to accidents, at risk for heart attack—but that didn't allay the worry that he had committed some sort of a crime. And what of his bloody nose? He hadn't the slightest idea why Wyatt had lashed out at him. And if he had? There was no getting around the fact that it looked as if there'd been a struggle here. Darkness congealed around him. His dog howled in the distance. Even now, Porter looked back toward the hall, half expecting to see Mrs. Hildebran emerging from the shadows, shaken but alive. He tightened his grip on the phone, imagined Franny across the street, her skin licked by candlelight, her blood aflame with ageless longing, and he was overcome with an incontestable foreboding that, after this, nothing would ever be the same.

"Are you there?" the operator said. "Is someone hurt?"

As quietly as he could, Porter set the receiver on the table and backed away. The call would be traced, the way he understood it. Someone would take care of Mrs. Hildebran. He wanted to find Wyatt Miller before the police arrived. They needed to get their stories straight.

Franny stared at her reflection in the window. The image in the glass was curiously unfamiliar and she realized, suddenly, that she had been avoiding her reflection ever since her haircut. She'd seen her face in mirrors, of course, brushing her hair in the morning, rubbing lotion into her cheeks at night, but she hadn't been looking, not really, and now that she was, she hardly recognized herself.

To the woman in the window pane, she said, "Why don't you just leave him?"

"He'd be lost without me," Rhonda said.

"You could go back to Texas by yourself. Wouldn't that be better than making a fool out of him?"

"He doesn't need me for that," Rhonda said. "You ought to know by now my husband has no trouble making a fool out of himself."

"Then why not cheat on him for real? Instead of pretending. Why not give him something serious to be jealous about?"

"Don't think I haven't thought about it," Rhonda said.

In the window, Franny watched herself finish the rum and Coke, watched her hand come up to rake the hair back at her temple. The tip of her nose was tingling slightly from the liquor and she reached out and touched its double in the glass. "It scares me to hear you talk like that."

Rhonda said, "How long you been married?"

"Three years this July," Franny said.

Rhonda made a sad and quiet sound, something between laughter and a sigh. There was a brief silence on the line. "You really don't know anything," she said. More silence. Franny was too startled by Rhonda's words to speak. After a moment, Rhonda said, "I gotta run. There's somebody at the door. I'll bet a hundred bucks Wyatt locked himself out again. That asshole forgets his keys like twice a week."

Porter was about to leave when the door opened, revealing Rhonda Miller in a black bra and red panties, holding a brass candlestick, the flame throwing jumpy shadows under her chin. Her jaw dropped and her eyes widened and Porter believed for an instant that there was something horrifying at his back. Then he understood that she was aghast at the sight of him and he covered his nose with his right hand.

"What happened?" Rhonda said.

Before he could answer, she gripped his elbow, hurried him inside, deposited him in a leather recliner in the den, and studied him with pained eyes, her navel swimming in candlelight.

"Wyatt did that, didn't he?" she said with conviction. "It looks like somebody hit you with a shovel."

"You're in your underwear," Porter said.

Rhonda laughed. "Too hot for clothes," she said. "No power, no AC."

"Where's Wyatt?" Porter said.

"You just sit a minute," Rhonda said. "Let me put a robe on and get some ice or something for your face."

With that, she turned and trotted toward the door, reaching behind her on the way out to flick the leg of her panties into place. It was clear to Porter that Wyatt wasn't home. He was still prowling the neighborhood. Porter pictured a brawny hunchback with insect eyes lurching from shadow to shadow, darkness rippling like water in his wake.

"Now then," Rhonda said, swinging back into the room, carrying a bag of frozen peas. Her robe was unbelted and Porter's eyes skimmed over her stomach. He could just make out an elastic imprint in the flesh above her panties. She sat on the arm of his chair and held the bag against his face, pressing him against the headrest. His pulse thumped in the bridge of his nose. Rhonda's breast was crushed against his bicep and, in spite of everything that had happened, he couldn't help feeling aroused.

"Is this about the dog?" she said.

Porter drew in a breath, as if to speak, then let it out. He didn't know how much to tell her. He wished he'd brought his cigarettes. It seemed impossible that Mrs. Hildebran was dead. He whimpered, involuntarily, and shut his eyes against the thought but he saw her crooked dentures in his mind and her sad, horrid legs. He opened his eyes again and there was Rhonda Miller peeking at him over the peas.

"I know," she said. "I know." Her voice was pitched low and tender like she was comforting a child. "What can I do to make it right?"

"I need to talk to Wyatt," Porter said.

Rhonda shifted her weight, causing the recliner to lower itself, dropping her into Porter's lap. Porter felt a stabbing pain in the side of his thigh. He rooted in his pocket, came up with Franny's earring, and dangled it between his face and Rhonda's. "Pretty," she said.

"It's Franny's," he said. Then, for no good reason, he added, "She wants us to have a baby."

"Tell me about it," Rhonda said, her lips close enough that he could feel her breath.

Franny phoned the power company and was informed by a recorded voice that due to the volume of inquiries, it would be an hour before her call could be received. She hung up and was struck at once by the silence in her house. It occurred to her that Tonto wasn't barking anymore and for all she knew hadn't been for some time. Her shadow leapt and broke against the wall.

"Vagina," she said, to dispel the quiet, "cervix, uterus, fallopian tubes," retracing the route of her husband's laggard sperm.

She took the candle from the counter and went to check on the dog, walking with her hips thrust forward, her weight on her heels, one arm slung over an imaginary belly, an imitation of the pregnant women she was always running into at the supermarket or the post office or the mall.

She hit the switch for the backyard floodlights, then shook her head at the mistake and opened the door. At first, she thought her eyes were playing tricks. She was drunk, after all, and there was no electricity. The night was only moon and shadow. Crouched in the yard was a hirsute, obscenely muscled, vaguely human figure, but where its face should have been, she saw a black mask with glassy eyes. From its mouth issued a kissing, coaxing sound. Tonto circled, rumbling softly, tail stiff as a wire. Neither of them noticed Franny. She brought a hand to her mouth and screamed, and, as if they had been waiting for just this signal, the creature and Tonto flew at each other, teeth bared in matching, vicious, prehistoric grins.

*   *   *

When he heard the scream, Porter was detailing for Rhonda the
sexual positions most likely to ensure fertilization, his eyes closed
under the bag of peas, Rhonda still in his lap, an unwanted erection pressing against his zipper. He bounced instantly upright,
dumping her to the carpet. "Jesus Christ," he said. "Did that come
from my house? Was that Franny?" He hurried through the Millers' dining room and laundry room with Rhonda at his heels, then
down the back steps and into the yard. He grasped the scene in
jump-cut fragments—Wyatt clamping Tonto in a half nelson, Tonto
squealing and flailing his paws, Franny pounding Wyatt's shoulders with a rake.

Without thinking, Porter hopped the fence, snatched the
rake from Franny's hands, clubbed Wyatt once, twice, three times
in the head, knocking the night vision goggles lopsided, before
Wyatt turned Tonto loose. Tonto slunk off behind the potting shed.
Wyatt came reeling to his feet. His gaze flicked over Porter's shoulder, a single exposed eye glinting now with reignited rage. Porter
turned and saw Rhonda climbing over the fence in her bra and
panties, her robe discarded on the lawn like molted skin.

"Wait a minute," he said. "Everybody just slow down a
minute now. We have to think what to do about Mrs. Hildebran."

Wyatt aimed a stubby finger at Porter. "You slept with
my wife," he said. He whirled on Rhonda. "Why him?" His voice
was wretched and high. "Look at him. He's nothing but skin and
bones." And, suddenly, with feeling close to relief, Porter understood what had happened in the dark at Mrs Hildebran's. He
watched Rhonda push a hand into her hair and puff her cheeks,
watched her eyes skip from Franny to Wyatt and back, waited for
Rhonda to dismiss her husband's accusation, but, to Porter's as-
tonishment, she exhaled and said, "I'm sorry, baby. I've been so
lonely here. All I wanted was for you to take me back to Texas."

"That's not true," Franny said, sounding, Porter thought,
more than a little drunk. "Rhonda, tell the truth." But Porter could

see that she was registering Rhonda's lack of clothes, grasping the fact that he'd come to her rescue by way of the Millers' house. He remembered his erection and blushed, his armpits simmering with shame.

"Don't listen to her, Franny," he said. "These people—" He stopped, trembling. He could feel the panic and frustration building in his chest. "That one scared Mrs. Hildebran to death."

"What are you talking about?" Franny said.

"He followed me over there and broke into the house—she must have had a heart attack."

"I don't understand what's happening," Franny said.

"I'm sorry," Rhonda said. "I hate this, Franny. You're the only good thing in the whole state of Alabama."

With that, as if his wife had just offered final, incontrovertible proof of her affair, Wyatt moaned and Porter saw him coming out of the corner of his eye—a burly shadow, a darkness not so deep as night. His teeth clicked with the impact of Wyatt hurtling onto his back. Porter wobbled, found his feet, careened over the grass. What came next happened too fast for him to process. Franny leaped on Wyatt and Porter sagged to his knees. Rhonda pounced on Franny and he collapsed. He wasn't sure if the women were trying to break up the fight or do each other harm. Wyatt went on panting in his ear, the sound feral and hoarse. Behind that, Porter heard Franny shrieking like some kind of savage bird, Rhonda cursing like dirty words might save her life.

In the next instant, his nerve restored, Tonto came charging out from behind the potting shed, bowled into the fray, and everyone was flung apart. Franny sprawled, gasping, on the lawn. Her tongue ached. She thought she must have bitten it during the struggle. She pushed onto all fours, fought back a wave of nausea. Her periphery was rimmed with gold and she didn't know if her distorted vision was a result of too much liquor or if she'd been knocked loopy in the fight. She saw Wyatt on his back, one arm across his eyes, the night vision goggles twisted around his neck. Rhonda lay on her side and coughed. Porter was still prone, his face buried in the grass. Franny crawled over and rolled him onto his back.

"Are you hurt?" she said. "Porter?"

His nostrils were rimmed with blood, his eyes dopey and lost.

"Mrs. Hildebran is dead," he said.

Tonto licked his face and Franny shoved the dog aside. She was in no state of mind for distraction or delay. Even her worry about Mrs. Hildebran seemed ages in the past.

"Get up," she said.

"I was afraid," Porter said. "I left her there."

"We need to get inside," she said. She hooked him by the armpits and heaved him to his feet and wrapped her arm around his waist. "We'll be safe inside," she said. They hobbled toward the house. Tonto followed, prancing a proud circle at their knees.

"I didn't know what to do," Porter said. "I've never seen anybody dead."

Just as they reached the door, Franny heard a keening sound. She looked over her shoulder and saw Wyatt Miller curled into a fetal ball, weeping into his hands. Rhonda snaked toward him on her belly, wrapped him in her arms, and rocked him like a baby.

In the kitchen, while Franny paced and wrung her hands, Porter told his wife the whole story. It didn't take long. When he was finished, Franny stopped and shook her head. "I don't believe it," she said. "This is not happening. How could all this happen in one night?" But Porter could hear the beginnings of comprehension in her voice. She touched her throat. Her fingers trembled. "Mrs. Hildebran?" she said. "My God."

Tonto threw himself down under the table.

"The police will be here any minute," Porter said.

As if to prove his point, siren lights flicked against the window. His gaze moved over Franny's face. She looked stunned and desperate. His legs were weak, his heart beating without rhythm, his blood still laced with adrenaline. Franny was crying now and he gathered her against him, intending to offer comfort, but before he understood what he was doing, he had kissed her throat, her jaw, her eyelids. He swept his hands along the backs of her thighs. "Don't," she breathed, "Porter, stop," but even as she spoke, she was fumbling with his belt. He lifted her onto the table. Franny clutched a handful of hair and yanked his head back and Porter winced.

"Rhonda?" she said.

"No," Porter said. "No, I swear."

Franny drew him between her knees, pressed her face against his neck. Her cheeks were slick with tears. Beneath them, Tonto beat his tail on the linoleum.

"I want a baby," Franny said.

Porter said, "We have to hurry."

"It's not the right time," she said. "It won't happen like this."

At that moment, the lights blinked on, the power restored, and he saw her face illuminated—her cropped hair, her frantic mouth. He almost didn't know her. Then the lights failed again, returning them to darkness.

"It'll be a miracle," Porter said.

Tonto scrambled to his feet and howled.

Acknowledgments

The author would like express deepest thanks to Jim McLaughlin, Hamilton Cain, and Murray Dunlap, great first readers one and all; to Adrienne Miller, Susanna Meadows, Roger Angell, Pam Durban, Lois Rosenthal, and especially Mr. Staige Blackford for shepherding these stories into print; to Elisabeth Schmitz and Molly Boren for editing nonpareil; to the Ucross Foundation and the University of Tennessee for time and support; to Warren Frazier for his patience and encouragement. And, always, with love, to Jill.